BECAUSE OF
YOU

BECAUSE OF
YOU

SUSAN HARRIS

authorHOUSE®

AuthorHouse™ UK Ltd.
1663 Liberty Drive
Bloomington, IN 47403 USA
www.authorhouse.co.uk
Phone: 0800.197.4150

Published by AuthorHouse   05/30/2014

ISBN: 978-1-4969-8263-6 (sc)
ISBN: 978-1-4969-8262-9 (hc)
ISBN: 978-1-4969-8264-3 (e)

ACKNOWLEDGEMENTS

I would like to say a big "thank you" to all of my readers who encouraged me to write a second book.

To Natalie J for the best feedback ever: this book is for you and for all my colleagues and friends who will be leaving soon. There are too many of you to mention by name, but I am indebted to you all.

To my new friend Peter: this book would not have been possible without your help. I cannot thank you enough.

And to all my new readers: I hope you enjoy it.

Thank you.

Titles by Susan Harris

I Promise You

CHAPTER ONE

Two months had passed by since Jack had seen *his* fiancée get married to someone else, and in those two months Jack had not moved on. He was still living in Autum's old apartment. He had bought it when she left and he had hardly changed anything in it. He was still sure that Autum would come back to him: it was not a case of "would she?" but "when?". He wanted her to know that he would be waiting for her, that she would not feel like a stranger in her own home. The only problem was that in the months since she'd left, Autum had started running a new office that had been set up by Frank and neither Jack nor Isobelle had seen her. The rumours were that her new office was based in Birmingham, a fairly new building called The Cube, with smart shops, bars and restaurants overlooking the canal. *Hmm... only a few hours drive or a nice weekend break...* Either way, he was going to "check out" these new offices for himself and he was going to take Isobelle with him.

Jack did have his regrets... in a weird way, his biggest one was that he had broken up the great relationship that Autum and Isobelle had built up over the last few years, a relationship that should never have been broken *over a man*. He had done that to them both and for that he was truly sorry.

He remembered that night just over three years ago now. He was out clubbing with the lads when he spotted the two sexiest girls there, one with long legs, a chest to die for and a figure most women could only dream of... and her friend, Isobelle, who rivalled her much the same. The only reason he'd ended up with Autum was that Isobelle had thrown herself at him and even though he was tempted, and boy, was he tempted, it was Autum's innocence that had grabbed his attention. For three years he had never once strayed or even looked at another woman. Then, a few months ago, Autum had started to have her "sleepovers", something that he'd encouraged her to do at the house with Isobelle. How ironic. *Something changed in me...* Jack had started to look at Isobelle in a different light. He always believed that he could look but not touch – "window shop" – but slowly Jack had realised that he wanted to look *and* touch. How stupid could he have been?

...At first it was the slightest things that Isobelle would do in front of me: a brush of her chest, the bending over then wiggling that ass of hers, the long seductive stare, the way she ate, drank. It just went on until the more she kept doing it, the more I found myself liking it. As far as I was concerned, it was harmless fun. After all, Isobelle was just a fun loving girl! The problem was that when Autum would go out for whatever reason, Isobelle would hit on me. She'd do silly things like throw cushions at me and we would end up play fighting. She'd jump on me until we were wrestling on the floor, her chest or her leg rubbing against me... she was turning me on and she knew it. But did I tell her to back off? What do you think – I'm a bloke aren't I! She enjoyed what she was doing, always knew the nights I was staying over and they always happened to be when she wanted a sleepover. I look back at it now and think she really did plan it all, but I also need to stop pushing the blame on her, it takes two to tango and I was more than willing. I wanted to have my cake and eat it, with both of them.

I do enjoy being with Isobelle. We're great together, she makes me laugh and I enjoy her company. In fact, I just asked her to move in with me. Sometimes, my mind strays though and when we're making love, it's Autum's face I picture in front of me. I've tried to move on, and I know that I need to move on, but I don't want to. I never realised how much I loved Autum until now, and now she's gone.

My father has summoned me for a showdown, that's what I'm sure it will be. I have been avoiding telling him that Autum's left me and married someone else. He's a shrewd man though, and I know that he must have heard rumours that I am now with someone else. He may be thousands of miles away but he knows almost everything: what I do, whom I'm with. I keep our conversations to business and when he asks about Autum I lie and say she's fine. I can see him on the screen casting that eye over me but I smile it off and change the subject.

When I told my father that I had proposed to Autum he was so happy, beyond happy in fact, as he worshipped the ground she walked on. He thought that she brought out the best in me and made me a better person. Little does he know the things I have done to her, the woman I loved and planned to marry. My father and Autum talked often on the phone and spoke via videoconference when she came to see me in my office. Sometimes I would listen to them both chatting away and realise how great they got on. He may be a hard man, but to see him relax while speaking to Autum was something worth seeing. She brought out his soft side as well as mine and she could even make him laugh, something he hardly ever does.

My father is well known in his circle, "a high flyer", you might say: very rich, very demanding and always gets what he wants. "Never back down," he used to say to me and I never did. A daddy's boy I will always be; I never wanted for anything and like him, I always got what I wanted. But how could I face him now, a failure in his eyes? I'd been the heir to a multi-billion pound industry but I had walked away from it, wanting to find a path for myself. Still, my father set up this company in England for me and left me to run it myself. With a turnover of five million a year and growing, at least I'm not that useless – Frank isn't the only shrewd businessman out there and I will prove that I have just as much to offer Autum as he does, as soon as I get a chance to see her.

I meet up with Isobelle for a drink after work and she tells me that Autum is due to attend an annual charity event with Frank and some of his associates on the twenty sixth of October. Even I know that these events are on a huge scale, and everyone who knows about Frank's events will want to be there; it's a place to be seen.

I take notice and pip up, this may be my only chance to see her again. Charity events can be open to anyone for the right price. I know Isobelle is missing Autum madly, even though she won't admit it. So I discuss this with her, saying that she can use this opportunity to make peace and try and rebuild some sort of relationship, if Autum is willing to give it a go.

Isobelle has been trying desperately to contact Autum since their split but Autum has now changed her mobile number, or rather, Frank has, and her emails keep bouncing back. She can't turn to Rebecca because whenever their paths cross at work, Rebecca blows her off with a killer look.

She must love the fact that she is now Autum's "best friend" when it still should be me. I have tried to break the ice by smiling at her but she blanks me. I know that I have no right to ask for any type of friendship or forgiveness from Autum, especially considering the way I went about things. I know she may still hate me for what I have done, but I miss her and I will do anything to prove how sorry I am for what I did. We have both moved on, her with Frank and me with Jack, and in a weird way, maybe she should be thanking me. After all it was me who brought them both together!

I remember the slap to the face I ended up getting, or should I say the fist, wow! She sure knew how to pack a punch, nearly knocked me off my feet. But I didn't hate her, knew she needed that release to move on. I accept that. I just want her back in my life. Emily and Dionne have kind of cut me off as well, always busy when I ask to meet up and cutting our conversations short when we do end up speaking. This is the price I've paid for stealing my best friend's man. But I won't give up – our friendship was tested and I failed badly, but I hope I can make amends when I see her at the charity event that Jack is taking me to... And yes, before you say anything, I know he still loves her. Three years together is a long time to just forget. I should know, Autum told me everything. I know he still feels some attachment to her through me, her ex-best friend. But I also know that I'm willing to wait until he wants me for me, until he doesn't just see me as a stopgap, something to fill the void.

I've loved Jack since the first time I saw him in the nightclub. Yes, I know I'd had a few – *ok I was totally paralytic* – but I wanted him then with the same passion as I have for him now. God, why did he fall for my best friend? And why could I not just be happy that Autum was dating him? Why? Because I was jealous. Because I saw him first. Because even though I did not say anything, the happier I saw them, the more I noticed that I wanted some of that. Am I a bitch, a man stealer, a person with no conscience? The answer is yes to all. All I know is that Autum is *my* best friend and *I will* get her back no matter what price I have to pay.

CHAPTER TWO

"Mrs Autum Howard". I still love the sound of my name when people call me, even though at first it took some time to get used to. I'd always look around to find out who Mrs Howard was! I look at my ring and realise how lucky I have been and how happy I am with the man I love, Frank.

The two months since my surprise wedding have flown by and I would do it all again. The looks on my mum and dad's faces were irreplaceable, and that reminds me, I still need to get Rebecca back for managing to hide it from me! I will give her credit for keeping it a secret though – I was clueless. Frank had a few more surprises up his sleeve whilst we were still out in the Bahamas. He produced a package with ribbons and bows all over it. I was so curious and when I looked up at him, he just said "For you." When I opened it, I saw this luxurious building, beautiful scenery, shops and bars. And as I continued looking through the photographs, I saw offices – fully decorated but empty. On the outside of the box, it just said, "The Cube, Mailbox, Birmingham". I looked up at Frank again and asked him if he was looking to move buildings.

He told me to continue looking through, which I did, wondering what Frank was going to do with this office. Then I reached the end. There was a picture of Frank and Rebecca with the biggest smiles on their faces and a placard that read, "To my wife, this is for you."

I stared at the picture, then looked up at Frank, stared at the picture once more, then looked up at Frank, then just stared into thin air trying to understand what this all meant. It was only when I felt Frank kiss me that I snapped out of whatever trance I had just put myself in.

"Do you like it?"

I started to stutter, "Is this for me?" I looked up at him.

"Yes. I want you to set up my new office in Birmingham; I know it's a few hours' drive but…"

"You did this for me?"

"My wedding present to you," Frank laughed. I gave my husband the biggest hug and kiss that I could give, before we headed back downstairs and met up with his parents for dinner. How time has flown since then!

I have taken a few trips to Birmingham since, to get to know my way around, and it is a lovely place – busy, but not as hectic as London. To get to the offices you can go through The Mailbox, where you can enjoy a quick bite to eat or do a bit of shopping. The Cube itself is something else, with offices, apartments, a gym complex and a restaurant with a three hundred and sixty degree view of the city. It sure is a breath of fresh air. I will like working here but, for now, I need to concentrate on recruiting and getting Rebecca to help promote job opportunities, as I would like to take a few staff with me to get the place up and running. If that wasn't enough, I also need to get a ball gown pretty quickly as I only have three weeks until the event! I call Rebecca for a catch-up and make arrangements for us both to go shopping as she is staying the week with me to help with the interview process.

We meet up in town and go to an exclusive shop that imports designer gowns for elaborate events. The first outfit I try on is royal blue satin: small trail, long sleeves and backless, so figure hugging I can hardly walk or breathe. Rebecca laughs as I start to waddle like a penguin. The second gown is a shocking red, high split and sleeveless and even though Rebecca loves this one, I'm just not feeling it. The assistant then pulls out a black silk, backless dress with lace bodice and sleeves, a small trail and a daring split at the front. As soon as I try this gown on, I know it's the one for me.

"Wow Autum," Rebecca laughs, "The men will be dribbling over you in that, and God help the jealous women accompanying them! You will not be a popular woman!"

"Rebecca, you're making me blush, stop it."

"It's just that you look so amazing! Frank will be the belle of his own ball," and with that, she gives me a hug.

I look again at this amazing gown and smile to myself – even *I* think I look hot. Rebecca decides to buy the red gown, let's hope that she gets a chance to wear it once Julian's seen it.

We head out for some lunch, spot an Italian restaurant hidden away in a little side street, and pop in.

I haven't been back to the London office since we came back from the honeymoon. Since Frank gave me the new office to manage, I have been so busy. In a way, though, it has been the boost I've needed, because to be honest I am unsure how I would feel walking back in there and seeing *her* and we all know the chances of that, don't we? Rebecca has never talked about Isobelle or mentioned her to me, which I am fine with... but then I think, "What is she not telling me? Is she hiding something from me?" I can't ask Frank, as he would flip, so I ask her anyway.

"So, how have things been in the office, Rebecca?"

"Busy, you know," she says, tucking into her appetizer of hand breaded calamari and our shared portion of chicken nachos. "I've moved desks now, have my own little office since my glowing report when we went away to Leeds."

"Wow! You never said," I reply, also tucking into the nachos.

"Well, I wanted to surprise you – knew I was seeing you today so I told Frank not to mention anything."

"Well you deserve it, girl." We continue eating, our main coming thirty minutes later. I've ordered shrimp Florentine and Rebecca is having the lobster ravioli and since the diet is out of the window for today, for desert I try turtle cheesecake and Rebecca has homemade tiramisu, followed by cocktails.

"Autum, stop giving me that look," says Rebecca, cautiously.

"What look?" I say, even though it was pretty obvious.

"What do you want to know?" she says with a sigh. For a second I nearly back out from asking her but if she doesn't want to tell me, all she has to do is say.

"Have you seen them?" She pauses for such a long time, sipping her drink, and eyeing me up. Then she speaks.

"Autum, don't do this, I promised Frank that I..."

"That you would what? Please Rebecca you know I will see them eventually. If you tell me what has been going on, at least it won't be a shock, will it?" Well if that guilt trip doesn't work, then nothing will... "Pretty please, I won't let on to Frank I swear."

"Ok, ok, enough already. Isobelle has moved into your old apartment with Jack. She's not in the admin department any longer – she's on the floor below us. When Frank got back from your honeymoon and found out, he lost it big time. And, last but not least, she's been asking to see you."

It takes a while to digest it all. I asked and now I got. *Isobelle and Jack together...* a slight pain goes through me but I don't know why. And why is she asking about me? *Maybe to rub it in.*

"Do you know what she wanted me for?" My breath sounds choppy as I speak.

"I think she wants to make up with you." I look up at Rebecca. I feel like I made her betray Frank's trust by telling me this and I owe her big time for it. I can see why Frank didn't want to tell me either, but I'm fine with the news – I'm happy for them – truly, I am. It just felt weird hearing it, that's all. And the last thing Rebecca said: *she wants to make up with me!*

"Are you ok, Autum?"

"Yes I'm fine, now let's have a drink and decide what accessories we need to go with our gowns." We both laugh and continue to talk for another hour before it's time to head back to the hotel and sift through some CVs before Monday's interviews.

Monday went by quickly but it was tiring. I had a team of ten people interviewing with me for different departments and it did not take long for the new building to be buzzing with life. The agencies we'd taken on board sent along some great potentials but if there's one thing I cannot stand it's when someone turns up in jeans: a big fat NO, first impressions count, remember!

I was interviewing fifteen people per session and there would be two sessions per day for the rest of the week. Those lucky enough to get through would then go onto an eight week training course. It was nearly lunchtime when Frank gave me a call.

"Hi Gorgeous, how's it going?" His voice is so soft and sexy I could just swallow him up through the phone.

"Good thanks, just tiring," I say. All I want is to hear his voice.

"Rosetta is missing you complementing her food as always."

I laugh, as Rosetta is an amazing cook, and feel my mouth watering at the thought of all the good home cooking that I'm missing.

"Well tell her that I'll be home soon and will be happy for her to overfeed me!" I can hear Frank laughing down the line. "Oh, and by the way Rebecca and I have bought our evening gowns and they should be delivered soon – no peaking when it arrives."

"Is it as sexy as the last one?"

I catch my breath, remembering Frank trying to pry me out of the dress and then waking up and seeing it torn to shreds. I take a few blinks and say, "It will be worth the wait."

"Umm that sounds interesting, I cannot wait." I have an image of Frank trying to picture me in whatever that mind of his thinks I'm going to be wearing. In his version, I doubt it will be much!

"How are things in the office?" I hear him pause and remember what Rebecca told me, (even though that was not why I asked) so I butt in again, "Any new work come our way?" And he answers me back in an instant.

As the week went on, it was great having Rebecca with me. It went by so quickly, we even still had our girlie nights in, sleeping in each other's rooms. How mad was that? It was so much fun and I knew that at the end of the week I would be heading back to London with her, back home and back to Frank. I'd been away for so long I could not wait to take some time out before the big event in two weeks.

As we packed up our belongings and headed for the station, it dawned on me that I would soon be home. We chatted for almost the whole train journey, talking about the ball, the interviews, work, going out, the people in our carriages and what they were wearing. Then we took some time out to read until we hit London and the busy lives we had left behind.

"Welcome home," I said to myself as we headed for a taxi, but to my surprise I saw a dashing man, or should I say, two, as Julian was there with Frank waiting for us. I forgot how sexy one man could be. I acted so girlishly – like I was meeting Frank all over again – and then I ran to him, dropping my bags and planting a smacker on his lips. Once his arms were around me, I forgot I was in such a public place and we kissed for what seemed like forever until I had to come up for air.

"I take it that you missed me, then?"

I started to blush as I could have taken Frank there and then I wanted him so much. "Can we go home?" I said in a rush, feeling a little bit embarrassed at how desperate I had just sounded. Frank whispered in my ear in his sexy voice,

"Hope you've built up an appetite as I plan to fuck you for hours..." Then he kissed my earlobe and I could feel his hot breath on my neck. I felt warm in all the right places – just the wrong location. I look around to see if anyone else had heard what he said, even though I knew they hadn't – the only people looking at me were Rebecca and Julian.

"Are you guys ready?" they asked, as I picked up my bags and headed for the car, trying to retain some dignity.

The traffic made the car ride seem long but I didn't mind. Frank and Julian kept bombarding me with questions, everything from the people who'd turned up for interviews to how the offices were taking shape. Boy, was I glad to be back... It was only when Frank started to stroke my leg and I looked across at him that I started to spot familiar surroundings. We would be reaching Rebecca's apartment soon and five minutes later I would be passing my old one. Frank was trying to reassure me. I put my hand on top of his to say that I was ok and smiled. My stomach was fine, I had no sudden urge to be sick, and no belly flutters; I truly was fine and I smiled inside to myself. We said our goodbyes to Rebecca and Julian and without thinking I said, "See you Monday!" Frank gave me *that* look, so I said, "See you soon!" and he smiled instead.

I cuddled up to Frank once they were out of the car and enjoyed the warmth of him beside me.

"Missed you," he said as he planted a kiss on my forehead. I looked up at him and said, "Missed you too."

Once we arrived home I took a step back to admire the house. It seemed as if I had been away far longer than I had but it was still a long time. I came out of my little dream world when I felt Frank's arm around my waist. "Are you ok?" He gave me that concerned look I had seen so many times when we first met. "Yes, I'm fine," I said and we headed towards the house. Rosetta gave me the biggest welcome of all time., how are you?"

"I'm very well thank you and please, call me Autum."

"Very well Mrs Howard, I have prepared some of your favourite treats for you. Would you like me to bring you some?"

Frank laughs, "It's been a long day and I think Mrs Howard needs to rest for a while." I give Frank a nudge as I can still see him smiling – I know Frank's version of "resting" and I'll be more than hungry later. I nudge him again as he is literally giggling the words as he speaks, *so mature.*

When we entered the bedroom, it was filled with red roses. He had even put petals on the bed, and there were scented candles all over. It smelt divine.

"It's lovely, Frank," I said, scanning the room. I entered the bathroom to see petals in the bath and the smell of lavender wafting up my nose, already making me relaxed. He must have asked Rosetta to do this *but when did he use his phone?*

"Only the best for my wife."

I told him that I could get use to this, must work away more often, as I turned to kiss him. After that, no more words were said.

Frank put a finger to my lips and shushed me, then slowly started to strip me piece by piece. Once he reached my underwear he stopped and looked at me, as if for the first time. I took that opportunity to do the same in return and left him in his D & G slowly undid the clasp of my bra and slipped the straps down. I took a breath when his thumbs brushed against my nipples, his hands working their way down my waist, his fingers slipping to the edge of my pants before he pulls them down. I follow his gaze and he never looks away from me. This sends my insides crazy. As he rises, he tickles me with his fingers. I try to wriggle free, he smiles.

I place my hands on his chest, the heat of him passing through me, his heartbeat increasing. I go around his back and place kisses on his spine. His chest moving forward, he tries to turn his head over his right shoulder, but I move it back with my hand and I hear him giggle. I tease him a little, moving my hand around his front, feeling the top of his underwear, slowly easing my hand in and touching the soft hairs below and letting them glide between my fingers. Then I slip my hand back out and pull down his boxers from behind, giving him a gentle slap on his bottom on my way up.

We both head towards the bath and slip into it, moaning as the heat sends that relaxing sensation though our bodies. I get comfortable, resting my head against his chest.

"Thanks Frank, this is so nice," I say, taking in the hot steam of the bath and the soft scent of the lavender. As he washes and gently strokes my hair, I close my eyes and start to drift off into my own world, Frank's voice slowly getting farther from my ears.

I see myself crying but don't understand why. I'm in a place that I am unsure of, a magnificent hall with elaborate fixtures and fittings and expensive artwork on all of the surrounding walls. There is a white grand piano in the middle of the room and crystal chandeliers hang from the ceiling. To the far end of this imposing space is a table that could fit at least twenty people. It looks like it has never been touched but all the place settings have been laid as if guests are expected. I wipe my tears away as I hear voices approaching the doorway. I pause for a moment then start to head towards it. I pass a mirror that takes up the space of a wall and stop when I see my reflection: a diamond crusted tiara is embedded in my hair, which is up and full of beautiful curls. I wear diamond earrings and a matching necklace and as I look down at my wrist there are diamonds there too. My dress, or should I say gown, flows freely to the floor and feels soft to the touch. I look at my reflection again, trying to touch the mirror to see who this person in front of me is. I hear the door push open and the sound of laughter. Then there are many people coming towards me as if I know them. The kisses start to flow as more people arrive and someone pushes a glass into my hand and fills it up. I sip from it as I take in the scene, wondering who these people are, why they are kissing me. I ask a silly question,

"What are we celebrating?" and a woman laughs.
"He said you were funny and he's right."
"Who said I was funny?" I respond, gulping another mouthful.
"Why, Jack of course, your husband."

I opened my eyes, startled and noticed that I'd jerked Frank as well.
"Are you ok? You looked like you needed that nap."
"How long did I drift off for?" was my response, as I sat up clearing the hair from around my face.
"Not long, a few minutes or so."
I started to hold the rim of the bath to ease myself out but Frank shot up behind me and got out first, water spilling around the floor. He went to grab my arm but I pulled back, as I took an intake of air. I tried to focus but I couldn't and the more I couldn't the more worked up I got.
"Autum, what is it?"
I started to shake – I could not see Frank in front of me, only Jack. As I came out of the tub, I could here the splash of water coming with me. Frank tried to hold onto me again but this time I panicked and as I tried to run away, I slipped. I heard Frank's voice calling out my name as I landed hard on my ass, my arms taking the impact. I just flopped the rest of the way to the floor, a shot of pain going through me. I lay there breathing heavily, tears running down the side of my face. Frank surrounded my body with his and wrapped a towel under my head telling me I would be ok. But would I? As all I could think was: Jack is back!!

CHAPTER THREE

I don't remember much after that. All I know is that I slept well, too well in fact, and woke up around eight in the morning. I call out for Frank and he appears out of nowhere and sits on the bed. I raise myself up as he tucks in the covers.

"Is everything ok?" I promised that I wouldn't hide anything else from Frank so I tell him what happened in the bath, spilling it all out in one go so that I don't lose my nerve. Then I look up at him.

"I think you should see a doctor." Frank's voice goes quiet.

"You mean a shrink?" I say, my voice starting to rise.

"I thought you had put all this behind you, what happened?"

Without thinking, I tell him what Rebecca had told me. When I look at him again he looks…mad, nope, I think that's generous. He is totally pissed, the sheets are being devoured under his grip, his face is about to explode and that look, well, I know either myself or Rebecca is about to meet our maker.

"Talk to me, Frank."

"She had no right to say anything,"

"I asked her to, don't blame her. Blame me, it was me who put her in that position. I was asking how things had been in the office while I had been away and I felt she wasn't telling me something so I laid the guilt trip on her and she told me everything, I won't have her take the blame."

What a way to wake up, with a sore ass and an argument – *great*. I slide out of bed and sit next to him.

"Frank, I will see them – you know that, don't you? It could be this week, next or in a month's time but I will see them so I need to know what's going on. You told me before 'no secrets', remember?" And with that, Frank nods his head. "Good, so I won't be sitting around here for the next two weeks, I'll be coming back to work."

"No way." Frank gets up from the bed all caveman-like to show his authority. I stand up too, to show him that I can be just as stubborn, then I wrap my arms around his neck and kiss him.

"Autum..."

"I won't take no for an answer." Then I walk off to the bathroom and shout, "See you downstairs!" before I close the door.

I missed Rosetta's food last night and am more than happy to make up for it with breakfast.

"Morning Mrs Howard," she says with the brightest of smiles and I return the favour.

"I have prepared your favourite things for you, anything else just give me a shout," and with that, she leaves the kitchen.

"Thank you," I quickly reply. As I tuck in, Frank joins me and we both eat. Looking round the room, I've forgotten how much I miss this, so I have decided that I will commute from now on. I've done all the ground work and everything is now in place.

"You know I've missed you so much?" says Frank.

"And I've missed you too. But you set me a challenge and I wanted you to be so proud of me. Plus I couldn't have concentrated on work if I had to come home every night to my sexy husband, now could I?" This makes Frank laugh.

"Any plans for today?"

"Well I'll be meeting up with Rebecca for lunch and *I* will tell her that you know everything and that you're cool with it." He raises an eyebrow but continues to eat.

"And then tomorrow you will be dropping me into work."

"Are you always going to be this stubborn?"

"Are you always going to be this sexy?" He goes to say something but growls instead. I take away his plate as he munches on his bacon.

"Hey, I've not finished yet!"

"Have you seen the time? Get to work and don't forget to call me." And with that, I get his jacket from over the chair and help him into it.

"Love you."

"Love you too," he says, walking out of the kitchen and towards the door. I hear the gentle click then quietness.

I meet up with Rebecca for lunch as planned and before I can say anything she blurts out, "You've told him haven't you?"

"What makes you think I said anything?" I'm trying to ease gently into confessing...

"Because he's been in a bad mood all morning, plus he keeps giving me the eye when he walks past. So, am I right?"

"Rebecca..."

"Oh Jesus, he's going to sack me."

"Calm down Rebecca, no he isn't. I told him that I would tell you myself. I did not mean for you to get into trouble but I had a bit of a turn last night."

"Turn? What do you mean 'turn'?"

"I had another dream when I was trying to *relax* with Frank last night. Ended up on my ass in the bathroom. Don't ask. After that I told Frank that Jack was back in my dreams and he freaked. Then I told him what you told me and he freaked even more."

"Thanks, Autum. You promised you would not say anything."

"And I meant it. It was only when I lost it that I told Frank everything you'd told me. I'm sorry, Rebecca. I will fix this I promise."

"I thought you were over him. I thought you had moved on."

"I had, I just can't explain what happened. And Frank wants me to see a shrink..."

"Maybe he has a point? What I mean is – your dreams are leading you down a path that can only be described as destructive. Nothing good seems to come out of these dreams, only hurt and pain. If a shrink can get you to understand them, then maybe they will disappear all together."

"I never thought about it like that. You may have a point, but the thought of talking about everything again, I'm just not sure I'm strong enough to deal with that plus the new office as well." I tell Rebecca that I'm due back in the office tomorrow and that Frank doesn't understand that I just *need* to do this.

"Jack means nothing to me and never will. I am so happy, I have the best girlfriend ever who's always watching my back and I have a function in two weeks to support my husband – I have to be ready."

"Are you ready? After what you have just told me...."

"More than anything."

Lunchtime goes by so quickly and before I know it, Rebecca is saying goodbye. I phone Frank soon afterwards but he doesn't answer because he knows that I will be pissed. *No matter, there's always tonight.* And with that, I go back home.

It was late when Frank arrived home, sneaking in like a child that was out later than their curfew, but I was waiting up for him, *in his study*. As he walked in to drop off his briefcase, I turned his chair around.

"Scared to come home now are we?"

"Jesus Autum, you trying to kill me?"

I smile but it doesn't last long. "I told you I would tell Rebecca in my own time but you just had to give her the killer looks, didn't you?"

"I don't know what you're talking about."

I shift out of the chair and head towards him wearing one of his shirts, bearing my legs and a bit of cleavage.

"Are you wearing.... my shirt?"

"Your shirt? I thought what was yours was mine?" *So much for me being mad at him.* "Do you want it back?" I look at Frank in the dim light and he starts to smile. Now he's heading towards me, his voice just a whisper.

"What do I need to do to get it back?" By this time we are chest to chest, I want Frank to take me now, in his study. His hands reach out and gently wrap around my neck to draw me nearer to him and we kiss, hard, demanding and passionate. This is what should have happened last night until I messed things up. This is what I had missed. Several times I try to catch my breath but as soon as I take a breath Frank is taking it away again. Then, without warning, I'm being swooped up, my legs wrapped around him for dear life, his hands firmly gripping my ass and heading straight for his desk.

"Frank! You'll wake Rosetta!" But it falls on deaf ears and the thought of getting caught turns me on even more. As he slams me onto the desk, he rips off his clothes and trips over as he tries to take off his trousers. I giggle as he pounces back onto me. He reaches under my shirt to find me with no underwear – he looks up and pauses.

"Is this what I get when I come home late?"

I sit up and try to pretend that I am mad at what he did to Rebecca,

"This is what you *would* have had, if you did not go behind my back and upset Rebecca." And then I jump off the desk and walk away with a smile on my face.

"You get back here, woman, or so help me God, I will fuck you for every step you take." Shocked, I turn around and look at this sexed-up wild man, mad with desire and ready to ruin me. I take a step back and he shouts out,

"One!" I stop. *God, he really means it,* he really is trying to burn me out, so why are his games driving me wild? I take another step back.

"Two! Do you really want to be worn out before work in the morning? I promise you will have *no* sleep tonight!" I try to run for the door but he's on me like a lion attacking its prey. We both fall to the floor, panting, and I let out a shriek, his body on top of mine.

"Going somewhere, Mrs Howard?" He slips one hand under my shirt and slowly moves up my inner thigh. I gasp, my blood pumping so hard for need of this man. He circles my clit with his fingers as I try to lift up my hips for him to go inside me but he just tuts at me. Round and round he goes, touching and teasing me.

"You're so wet Mrs Howard..." He inserts two fingers inside me and I moan. He licks my earlobe and whispers, "Are you ready to be fucked?" and I feel myself getting wetter, *I'm such a nasty girl,* and my legs getting wider, ready for this man. Then I feel air as he pulls out, gets up and walks away, his cock hard and bouncing up and down as he heads back to his desk.

"Frank, is something wrong?" I say, panting, and head towards his desk.

"Are you still mad at me for what I did to Rebecca?" His back is facing me but I know he's smiling. Damn, he's having the last laugh, playing me at my own game. I'm horny as hell and now I will have to beg for his forgiveness, but beg I will...

"Sorry Frank, I just wanted to make a..." He's on me again as I fall back onto the desk, gripping the edge for dear life. My butt's barely resting on the edge when his fingers enter me again. He pumps me harder, his thumb working my clit. I raise my hips again and he inserts another finger as my head lulls back with the sheer pleasure. He grabs my nipple, bites and sucks – I come, but he gives me no time to recover. Still throbbing from my orgasm, he puts his cock inside me, my juices sucking him all the way in. Hard and fast he enters, in and out, his balls trying to damage me into surrender, the sweat dripping down from us. He kisses me deep like his cock's in my mouth, matching his thrusts. He grabs hold of my hips and penetrates me even deeper, filling whatever space is left before he looses himself in his own orgasm, giving me all that he has inside him until it's gone, then wrapping me up around him so that we can both catch our breath.

The morning arrives and I am pumped up for two reasons: last night of course and the fact that I will be heading back to work. I get up and hit the shower, joined quickly by Frank.

"Are you ready for today?" he says in a worried tone.

"Of course I am, stop worrying. If anything goes wrong you will be the first to know I'm sure."

We head down for breakfast and Rosetta mentions that she has tidied up the study. The shame hits me and my face glows red. Frank just laughs when I nudge him in the side.

"Sorry Rosetta, things got a bit rough last night!" I nudge him again, as he giggles into his tea.

"No need to apologise, Mr Howard, you are still newlyweds after all!" Then she looks up and smiles at us both. I cough up my breakfast, spraying the table. All Frank can do is laugh and all I can do is bow my head into my plate. It's definitely my cue to leave. I quickly say my goodbyes to Rosetta and tell Frank that I'll meet him in the car as he continues to laugh.

Frank was chuckling all the way to work and in the end I had to join him. It was a great way to start my day and to prepare me for walking through those doors. As I stepped out of the car, Frank gave me the longest loving kiss. It was what he needed to do to reassure me that I would be ok.

I said my hellos to Janice and Bob in reception. As they passed on their congratulations, I headed to my desk on the fourth floor. At first I felt a few pin pricks walking through, but everyone made me feel so welcome. Rebecca greeted me and walked me to my desk and after showing off my wedding ring for the umpteenth time I booted up my computer and got straight into work. By ten o'clock it was as if I had never left the building – emails upon emails just waiting for responses. That was good; it kept me busy.

"Congratulations, Autum."

I didn't need to turn round to know that voice belonged to Isobelle. At first I wasn't sure what to do but I decided to turn and face her. This, ladies, was how I'd always pictured a female Judas – loyal and loving but happy to stab you in the back at a moment's notice, then thinking that by asking for your forgiveness, everything would be hunky dory. *News flash, Isobelle, Judas did not have a happy ending!*

"Thanks." I'd never seen Rebecca move so fast. As she approached, Isobelle held up her hands and said, "I'm leaving, back off."

"What did she want?"

"She just passed on her best wishes...?"

"Don't let her back in, Autum." I stood up and put my hand on her shoulder.

"Don't worry, that will never happen." As I looked over Rebecca's shoulder, Isobelle glanced back at me, then continued to walk.

I was late taking my lunch but I met up with Rebecca, Julian and Frank for a quick bite to eat at Subway and updated Frank on my morning. When I went back to work there was a huge parcel on my desk. I looked around and asked my colleagues who had left it and they just said it was delivered and brought up from reception. As I opened the box, I could see long stem white lilies and a bottle of Bollinger. I looked for a note and found it between the flowers. It read, "To Mr and Mrs Howard, wishing you a long and happy life together, Love, Jack and Isobelle x"

As colleagues again gathered around my desk, including Rebecca, the only thing I could do was to ring Frank and tell him.

Jack knew how much I loved white lilies and that Bollinger was indeed my favourite drink but you know I felt nothing when I saw both their names in the card. I picked up the phone and rang Isobelle to thank them both for our gift then hung up before she could reply.

When my day finally finished, I was glad to just kick off my shoes and relax. I put the lilies in the hallway and put the champagne on ice. As Frank said to me earlier, "Why waste a good bottle?" And he was right, why waste it indeed?

CHAPTER FOUR

After my first week, things had settled down nicely and I wanted to meet Imogen, Emily and Dionne as I had not seen them for a few months and the ball was only around the corner. Frank said that they could all come back to mine, so I decided to arrange a movie night in. Everyone would wear a onesie and a gift would be given for the most unusual onesie worn.

I mentioned my theme to Frank, who pointed out that it was going to be a challenge on my part as onesies are not something that I normally wear. I trawled through websites to come up with an outfit and was happy with my choice – I just hoped it would arrive in time.

Rosetta had prepared a feast for my friends and Frank was going out with Julian for a lads' night out, which was nice. As Frank kissed me goodbye, he told me to get as drunk as possible and I knew where his mind was heading. After he left, I rearranged the living room, got the movies ready, laid out all the food and lit the candles. The scene was set and all I needed were the girls.

At eight thirty, the doorbell rang. Frank had organised a lift so that all the girls came together. Rosetta greeted them and showed them into the living room – they were taken aback by the size of the place.

"Wow! This is great, Autum," said Imogen, who was wearing a Panda onesie. Emily was in her Barbie onesie, Dionne in her Wonder Woman onesie and I was in my Mini Mouse onesie. We all had a laugh and took some photos, posing as if we all had superpowers. I gave them a tour of the house and showed them all which rooms they would be sleeping in, if we made it upstairs by morning that is.

We microwaved the popcorn, ate all of the snacks that Rosetta had prepared and then opened the wine (lager for Imogen), popped in our first movie, *The Hunger Games*, and settled in. Bottle after bottle was opened and can after can was pulled by Imogen and the movies just kept flowing. I excused myself at one thirty to get some air. As I took in a breath and the cold hit my face, everything started to spin. Why I thought having another swig of my drink would help I don't know, but I quickly thanked the lord for the great night I was having before heading back into the house and joining the girls.

When we were all too drunk to focus anymore, we just sat up and talked.

"Do you think you and Frank will have children?" Emily asked.

That took me a little by surprise, as we had not talked about starting a family. At the lodge he had taken me to, he had mentioned that he would love to have children, but that he had not found anyone he wanted to settle down with. So I just said, "When the timing is right."

Rebecca piped up and told everyone that she would, of course, be godmother and a bout of laughter went around as the girls called her "Barbie godmother".

We talked about the charity ball that was happening the week after, and both Emily and Dionne started to snigger.

"What's so funny?" Rebecca asked.

"Oh nothing," said Dionne and with that puzzle we changed the subject.

"Did you tell the girls what Isobelle and Jack bought you as a wedding gift when you came back into work," said a giggly Rebecca.

The shock announcement made the room fall deadly silent, with all eyes looking at me.

"Bought you?" said Imogen, who now seemed to have jumped out of her drunkenness.

"They bought me some flowers and champagne, no biggie," I said, trying to shrug it off.

"Does that mean that you and Isobelle are friends again?" said Emily.

It was getting uncomfortable for me now, and I did not want it to spoil my night so I ended this line of questioning once and for all.

"My friendship with Isobelle ended when I found them both having sex in my apartment and in my bed. My friendship with Isobelle ended when Jack attacked me twice and she defended him and not me. So if you still need to ask me if me and Isobelle are friends then you are obviously not drunk enough." And with that, I raised my glass and drank the contents, even though they tasted bitter sweet.

I knew the girls were mumbling about the conversations when I went to put some of the empty bottles in the kitchen. It would have been unfair of me to leave the place a total mess for Rosetta and when I re-entered into the room that eerie silence followed.

"Sorry Autum, we didn't know," was Emily's response.

"I've moved on," was mine and the matter was closed.

When did I fall asleep? I have no idea but I am sleeping. I remember being asked about children and that thought made me look at my life differently. I pictured having the family round our house for our first Christmas together: Frank so excited that his parents are flying in from the Bahamas to spend it with us, unsure if the fact that I was expecting twins helped them book that ticket. A boy and a girl they'd told me and I was going to call them Crystal and Nathan. It was all planned in my head. I'm enjoying this dream when I feel my body moving. I strain one eye open to see Frank picking me up.

"What are you doing? What time is it?" I say in a whispered voice, as I see the girls burnt out on the floor covered in blankets. "Did you do that?"

"I was trying to make them a bit more comfortable. Hope you don't mind. And the time by the way is four fifteen in the morning."

"Have you just come in? Did you have a good time? You don't seem drunk?" I fire the questions simultaneously.

"Yes to all of your questions except the last one. I wanted you drunk remember." He continues to carry me up the stairs.

I slowly focus on our room. "Frank, we have guests downstairs! You can't expect me to make love to you!"

"No, you're right – I don't expect *you* to make love to me..." I sigh with relief but before I can reply, he adds, "I will be making love to you. So if you don't want your girlfriends to hear how loud you can be, you better practice your breathing." He tells me to relax and with that, he laughs, but all I can think is – *Hell no.*

I curl up in bed with my back away from him and he gives me a hug. With his body heat and this damn onesie I feel like a hog roast. I know he's awake and that he is waiting to eat his prey but I am determined to hold out, wishing sleep will hit me once again. After a while, I can't breathe I am that hot. Fleece onesies are, I have to admit, the best for sleeping in on a cold winter's night but winter has not hit us yet and I need to slip out of this once I know he's asleep. What feels like an hour slips by and I can hear his deep breathing. I thank the gods, slip out of bed and take off my onesie, slipping into something lighter and cooling down instantly. I turn back round to return to bed and see a shadow in front of me. I scream but it's only Frank.

"What the fuck! I thought you were sleeping, you scared the shit out of me!"

"When will you learn, Mrs Howard, that you husband has always been a light sleeper?" His lips curve to the side.

With my heart still pounding I get back into bed, now unable to sleep, and still drunk. He nibbles on my ear and I ignore it. He licks my neck and I start to fidget. Then he grabs my breast and starts to pinch my nipple and I start getting hot. *I'm so weak.*

"Shall I stop?"

Now he asks *that* question. My back is still away from him but I can feel his friend poking me from behind. I turn around and he kisses me. *That's all it took...* I turn him on his back and wrap my hand around his cock, his veins pumping in my hand. It's then I realise he's completely naked. *Now he's a magician,* I say to myself

I tell him to get off the bed and stand up. I kneel down and put my hands behind my back as if they were tied up and tell him to feed me. As I open my mouth, he guides his cock in and supports my head. God, he was solid before I started to suck him. Talk about loud – he is moaning gyrating, pumping and all the time asking me if he's hurting me. I shake my head to say no and he continues. This is for him, I want him to fully let go. I slap him hard on his ass and I can feel his arousal in my mouth so I slap him again even harder. His speed is building and so is the noise he's making. I want to laugh but I will remind him of that later. As he continues to pant and his breathing becomes more choppy, I know I have to prepare myself, and when I hit him one last time he explodes in my mouth, screeching, shaking and breathing uncontrollably all at the same time. I drift off to sleep not long afterwards and wake up earlier than expected at nine thirty. When I shower and go downstairs, the girls are still out for the count but Rosetta is in the kitchen cooking up a storm of a breakfast for us all. Frank is already up and about and in his study working so I pop in just to say "Hi".

"Sleep well?" I ask.

"Like a baby, thanks to you."

"I know this may be bad timing but can I have a quick chat?"

Frank swivels his chair at record speed and is by my side before I can utter another word.

"What's wrong?"

"Nothing really but the girls asked me a question last night and I didn't know how to answer it."

"Go on..."

"They asked me if we would be having children." Frank kisses me and takes me back to his chair and I sit on his lap.

"So what did you say to them?"

"Just that we will have them when the timing is right."

I look at Frank for some response, but he just ponders.

"Sorry, I shouldn't have bothered you." I try to get up.

"Where do you think you are going, Mrs Howard? You did not give me a chance to respond."

"I just thought..."

"That I didn't want them? You know I do – we talked about this before we were an item."

"I know but we've never discussed children since we've been together."

"Are you saying that you're ready to have our children?"

And there it was – that fifty thousand dollar question.

"Yes I am."

I hear the girls calling me and I kiss Frank and leave him to work. I help Rosetta get the food ready and we all sit round the breakfast bar to eat.

"Never again," says a red-eyed Imogen.

"Second and third that," say Emily and Dionne as I laugh.

"How come you look so perky?" says Rebecca, "Oh, I know you've got that sex in the morning face on."

I blush as they all look up at me.

"Yep, she left us last night to have sex, guilt written all over her face!" And the fact that I'd smiled back said it all.

"So dirty," Rebecca replies and we all laugh as we continued to eat.

Frank comes in and joins us, maybe at the wrong time and Rebecca mumbles, "Look at that sex face." Bubbles of laughter are coming from the girls' juice glasses.

"Ladies, if you are not too busy, would you all like to join us for lunch?" I look up at Frank and give him a wink. This is a nice surprise and the girls think so too and are all happy to agree.

"Don't worry, Rebecca, I have invited Julian around as well." They all look at me and I shrug my shoulders – I am just as taken by surprise as they are.

"Do we have enough food?" I ask.

"You know I always stock up," replies Rosetta and gives me a smile.

When Frank retired back to his study, I popped my head around and caught him on the phone to his parents talking about children. He looked so happy for what the future might hold. He ushered me in and I sat on his lap again. I said "Hi" to them both and chatted for a while then left them to it and joined the girls again.

"Frank seems in a good mood."

"He is, we talked about having children this morning." A beaming Rebecca tries to hug the air out of my body.

"I'm so happy for you both!"

"Well, we've not said when we would try, just that we are both ready." The more I mentioned children, the more comfortable I was getting. "Anyway, we still have a lot of things to do before that happens. I need the new office to be fully operational, go on a healthy diet and cut out the booze." *I've got my work cut out over the next few months but it will be worth it.* The only other concern that most women have is that until you start trying for a baby, you don't know if you can have them.

I change my trail of thought and look forward to having my close friend here for lunch. As Julian arrives, I help Rosetta with the setting of the dining area even though she tries to protest – I won't have her doing everything herself. As we gather around for lunch we talk about life, family, business and the new offices in Birmingham. By the time we've finished, it's well after five in the afternoon and the girls start to call it a day.

"Thanks for a wonderful sleepover, Autum. Definitely need to do this again, but at my house next time," says Dionne.

"Will take you up on your offer, just let us know when."

"Will do," and we kiss goodbye and then the noise disappears.

I'm shattered after my night and day and I lay on the sofa for a nap. Before I've blinked I'm out for the count and dream about the great day I've just had. But then my dream takes another path.

I'm riding in a sports car, laughing, my hair blowing in the wind. I ask where I'm going but get no reply. I'm dressed elegantly, with designer glasses on my face. After an hour's drive we stop and I'm surrounded by convertible Bentleys, Rolls Royces, chauffeured cars – you name it, it's here. But as I step out of the classic TVR I hear "click, click, click". My photo is being taken, I'm at a polo match. It's a hot day and the sun is beaming down on me. After the first match, we retreat into the tent to have a five course meal followed by glasses upon glasses of champagne. I have baronesses to my left and wealthy yacht owners to my right. We raise a toast to the table and I turn to kiss... Then a loud thud.

I woke to find that I had turned on the sofa and fallen off; Frank was trying to hold back a laugh while Rosetta looked concerned. *At least someone was.*

"What happened?" Frank said in his *I'm trying my best not to laugh* voice.

I got up, fixed myself and sat back on the sofa, ego intact.

"Obviously enjoying my sleep too much," I said, trying to end the conversation quickly.

"Would you like me to fetch you something?" asked Rosetta.

"I think she may need a bigger sofa" was Frank's reply, a chuckle leaving his mouth.

I raised my eyebrow and shook my head.

"If you've finished with the jokes, I'm fine Rosetta, but thank you for being the *only* one concerned for my wellbeing." I looked at Frank as I was speaking.

"I'm sorry darling, but you must admit, it *was* quite funny." Yet another chuckle left him. To be fair, it was funny, but I didn't want to give him the satisfaction that deep down, I was laughing my head off.

CHAPTER FIVE

By the time I stepped into the office on Monday, not only was I the coolest person to host a movie night in, but I was also apparently pregnant. Office gossip is one of the quickest and least reliable ways to make things up. By the time it's left one mouth and the Chinese whispers have started, the results can end up better than a movie.

I call Rebecca on the phone to find out where these rumours are coming from.

"Some of the girls asked me how my weekend was and I just said that we had a great time at yours and then we started talking about having children."

"Rebecca, how could you? Everyone thinks I'm pregnant! You need to fix this big time, I don't want Frank to think this is all coming from me."

"No problem Autum, by the end of the day you'll wonder what all the fuss was about."

I hang up the phone and try to concentrate on all the work that seems to be piling up; the more I clear, the bigger the pile gets.

"I hear congratulations are in order."

Whore bitch. I stand up so that the office can see that I am not pregnant.

"Your congratulations are a bit premature because I am not pregnant."

"Oh, I heard..."

"Yes I'm sure you did, along with the whole building, but it was just a big misunderstanding. People make one plus one equal three – you know how it is."

"Sorry, but I think you will make a great mother," she says and walks off. I grind my teeth as I sit back down. Cheeky bitch, how the fuck would she know? The only thing Jack *claimed* she was good at was screwing someone else's man.

I continue to work, slamming hard on my keypad. *Why does she always appear? She's worse than a God damn leech.* I decide that Isobelle is obviously getting the wrong idea from me because I have been speaking to her. The only reason I am doing it is because I am at work and even though she is testing my temper, I will always be polite and professional.

I miss lunch, as I don't have the stomach to eat, *which will give them something else to talk about.* I tell Frank that I will get a cab home late, as I need to catch up with my work.

It's eight thirty by the time I get my coat and bag and head towards the lift. I reach reception. Janice and Bob have left and a stand-in security guard has taken over. I smile, head through the doors and phone a cab.

"Ten minutes? Didn't think you would be that busy on a Monday night. Ok, just hurry."

I phone Frank and tell him that I am just waiting for a cab, even though he offers to come and pick me up. The night air is fresh and the traffic seems to be quieting down. I pace up and down the pathway as I don't want to go back and wait in reception.

"Hello Autum..."

I knew this day had to come sooner or later, but hearing his voice, I just couldn't prepare myself. I turn round and there he is standing in front of me: Jack. I stop and look at him. I can't speak or focus, I just keep staring. He's grown a bit of stubble that makes him look even sexier. His hair style has completely changed too – it suits his look. His scent is just as seductive as I remember it.

"Jack..." that's all I can say as he sweeps me up with his eyes. I'm being hypnotised and I can't help myself.

"You're looking well," he says, "Did you receive my gift?" *He said my gift not our gift.* I hear a "beep, beep" and realise my taxi has arrived.

"It was beautiful, thanks. I loved it. I mean, we both did. Got to go, bye."

"Bye, Autum."

I turn around to take one last look at him before I get into the taxi. It's only then, when I snap out of whatever you could call what just happened, that I think, *what the hell have I just done?*

By the time I got home I was too drained to talk, never mind eat. I made my excuses and went to bed.

Jack couldn't believe his luck. Something had told him to take a stroll without Isobelle and that's what he'd done. He'd been drawn to walk by the offices that they worked at and now he felt like he had just hit the jackpot.

When he saw someone pacing up and down the pavement, he knew they were waiting for either a lift or a taxi. Then he recognised those sexy long legs and that hairstyle and he knew it was Autum. He didn't want to scare her, just wanted to say "hello". He needed to know how she would react to seeing him again after such a long time. He paused at first and felt his shoulder where she had stabbed him – a painful reminder of what he had done to her, *never to be forgotten.* He had thought of numerous different scenarios in his head of how this could go down. Would she scream and get some random passer-by's attention? Would she run for dear life, saying that he was following her? Or would she just attack him again? He just didn't know. Whatever the case, he needed to find out.

When he said the simplest of words and she turned around, her beauty was even greater than he could have imagined. She was flawless to him and he felt a pain in his chest. On seeing her it confirmed what he knew in his heart: he was still in love with her. He noticed she was stunned to see him but she wasn't rude. To him, that was more than he could have hoped or wished for: a sign that she didn't hate him. And when she turned around before getting in her taxi, there was not a hint of anger in those beautiful eyes.

Jack took this to mean that they could be friends once more. He convinced himself that the only person that could stop that from happening was Frank. Frank was the problem, not Autum. He felt his hand fisting into a ball as soon as he mentioned his name and took a deep breath to relax. He slowly continued his walk for another ten minutes, his mind working overtime on the night's events, before heading back to his apartment. His mood had lifted and he whistled all the way back. He was going to make love to Isobelle as soon as he got in, with Autum's face freshly in his mind.

I had gone upstairs to take a shower and to relax. I lay on the bed and went over the night in my mind. I remembered Jack saying "hello" to me, Jack's seductive voice, and how sexy he seemed with his new look. *Why would I feel like that towards him? Haven't I suffered enough? Why didn't I just scratch out his eyes, the bastard? Why?*

Where inside me was this new demon coming from? I preferred when my subconscious mind was pushing me to be with Frank. *I should never have spoken to him, but he reminded me of the old Jack I knew and my body responded to him. How cruel.* I wished myself to sleep so that I could forget, but before long I started to dream...

I was choking, finding it hard to breathe. There was a funny smell but my nose did not know what it was, only that I was trying to fight it. I heard glass shattering. Then everything went dark...

I'm shocked when Frank wakes me to get up in the morning. *Did I really sleep that heavily?* Feeling groggy, I get up and head for the shower.

"I think work is getting too much for you," says Frank, as he joins me in the shower.

"I'm fine. It was probably me working late, trying to catch up on my work that did it." I try to act as jolly as I can as he washes my back. I decide then that maybe I do need to book an appointment to see the shrink.

"Do you have that number for the, err, shrink you suggested?" His hands pause for a moment.

"Has something happened?"

"No," *the guilt killing me,* "I have just been thinking about seeing a shrink."

"Doctor," he corrects.

"As I was saying, it might be good for me to talk to someone professionally and get their intake on why I seem to be having these dreams again."

"Again? You mean you've been having more?"

Oh shit. My big mouth and me... "What I meant was, I haven't had that type of dream for the last two months and I don't want to have them again. If the 'doctor' can help me then why not?" He turns me around and kisses me, *not helping when I'm trying to get myself ready for work.*

"Thank you," he says.

"For what?" I ask, before he pins me to the wall, a shower far from his mind.

I tell Rebecca what I've decided to do over lunch and about the encounter with Jack last night.

"OMG Autum! What the hell?"

"I know and I don't know myself what happened. Just that I just couldn't think straight..."

"I need to ask you this question, Autum. Do you still have feelings for him?"

I pause for a moment.

"What about Frank?"

"I love Frank, you know that."

"So why the fuck did you pause when I asked you that question? After everything he did to you AND ME, you still feel something for him? Christ, Autum, you really do need to see that fucking shrink." She storms off from the table and leaves me.

I look around to see if anyone else from the office has just witnessed our little outburst in the café but luckily no one is there. I feel a fool and a total idiot. I know I don't have any feelings for that sick bastard but the demon inside me refuses to let me say it. *He's winning.*

I head back to the office deeply upset, and worried that I may lose the only person I can confide in. Even worse, she might tell Frank. I ring her several times but she refuses to take my calls. I decide that she needs some space. How could I have forgotten that I obviously brought up some bad memories for her as well? *How foolish of me.* I will try and speak to her tomorrow. I go into the break area and dial Dr P Hillard's number. He is quite accommodating and I'm pleased that he can fit me in on such short notice. My appointment is for three forty five tomorrow. His voice is soft and pleasant but I picture him as short, balding and in his mid to late forties. I chuckle to myself and then head back towards my desk.

Thursday arrived and I was getting slightly apprehensive for my afternoon. I did not really know what would happen and I think that was what scared me the most. How far would he expect me to go? I shivered at the thought but I had promised Frank that I would give it a go. Rebecca had not spoken to me since and that was concerning. I saw her every day and that day was no different but she looked straight past me as if I wasn't there. I send her a note when she slips out of the office saying "Sorry" with kisses. I did not need to sign my name as she would easily recognise my handwriting.

I see her approach her desk and pause. I know she knows I'm watching her and I try to look away discreetly. *No response.*

I go to my local café alone and sit down with my sandwich. I take a few bites and I hear the chair in front of me screeching.

"Is this seat taken?"

Has this bitch got a death wish or what? I ignore her and tuck into my Italian flatbread sandwich but she sits down anyway.

"Are you following me now?" I say with a mouthful of bread.

"Yes."

I'm so shocked at the statement I freeze with the food still in my mouth.

"This may be the only time I get to say what I need to say without your 'bodyguard' ushering me away, so here goes. I cannot undo what has been done nor do I want to. You have been my friend for such a long time and I get that you're still pissed at what I did. I get it, truly I do, but I miss you Autum. I really do. If you want me to say sorry a thousand times I would. I know we can never be like we were before, but if you would at least smile at me or say hello and truly mean it, that would be a start."

She stops and looks at me for a response, my food now wedged in my throat trying to choke me. Every time I try to swallow, it feels like it's swelling and cutting off my windpipe. I take a swig of my drink to loosen it and it goes down. What made me do what I did next? Well maybe I can only be described as a volcano that had been dormant and was now ready to erupt.

"You have the fucking nerve to sit next to me acting like you took a cookie from my jar without asking. Not only did you fuck my fiancé when I was working away but you had been fucking him for months before that, laughing in my face but fucking him behind my back. How dare you then sit here and ask me to say hello and smile after what you did? Don't you get it, bitch, I want you to leave me the fuck alone. What do I have to do to make you understand that? I hate you, Isobelle! I hate you!" I start to cry and throw my food and drink at her as she gasps. I then make sure she gets the message and slap her hard across the face.

"Does that make my feelings clear?' I run out of the café.

By the time I was out of view, I had broken down. This was not going to be good for me at work. Why did she do it? Why did she push her God damn luck? Even I knew I might have gone a step too far. *Should I go back and apologise?* I was seriously thinking about it but decided to continue back to work until I felt a sharp tug on my arm and was swung round.

"Jack," was the only word that came out of my mouth; *he must have been on his way to meet her.* He was standing next to a very wet, Italian smelling Isobelle who was putting on the waterworks in front of him and holding onto his arm.

"Is this how you treat her after it took all her courage to apologise to you? Is it?"

"I did not ask or want her apology. I just want you both to leave me the hell alone and get on with your own lives. And don't touch me Jack. EVER. I may have dropped the charges before because I thought you would have learnt your lesson, but lay a finger on me now and I will have them hall your ass into that station before you can blink. And what would dear old daddy think of his precious son then?" *Sometimes, when you're angry you should be very careful what comes out your mouth unless you are prepared to face the consequences.*

I felt myself being slammed against the wall as Jack grabbed me by the throat.

"Jack!" Isobelle screamed, "What the hell are you doing? For God's sake, she didn't mean what she said! Did you?"

How the hell she expected me to reply with Jack's hands around my throat, I don't know. I couldn't have nodded my head even I'd wanted to and despite the situation I was in I was not going to apologise. Then he whispered in my ear,

"I will crush everyone and everything dear in your life for what you have just said. You don't know what I'm capable of, do you?"

I put both my hands around his to try and loosen the grip and croak out my response.

"Rape, Jack, that's what you are capable of. Remember?" When the words finally register in his brain, he lets go, instantly. I bend my head forward and rest my hands on my knees, coughing.

Isobelle tries to console me, *can you believe that,* but I shrug her off.

"Well at least she can see your true colours now, Jack"

"Autum, I'm so sorry." He bends down and tries to put his hands around me but I recoil.

I did not give him the pleasure of seeing how scared I was. Once I got my breathing back to some sort of normality, I straightened up and ran in the direction of a taxi rank.

I cried all the way home and continued to cry once I was inside, as Rosetta rushed to my aid.

"What has happened, Mrs Howard?"

I caught my breath and told her that I was fine.

"I will call Mr Howard."

"NO!" I shouted, "He must not hear of this. Understand?"

"But you are distraught, you look a mess. I cannot lie to him if he asks me. Have you been... attacked?"

Instinct made me nearly reach for my throat but I pulled back.

"Please Rosetta, please, I will be fine, I promise." I tried to smile it off which was so unconvincing even Rosetta rolled her eyes at me.

"You put me in an awkward position, Mrs Howard," she said, walking away.

It is now two thirty and my appointment with Dr Hillard is in just over an hour's time, but I'm in no fit state to see anyone. I look at my neck to see if there are any marks: a bit red, but nothing that should not fade. I'm more worried about whether Rosetta will tell Frank. *All I want is a stress free life, is that too much to ask?*

I cannot cancel my appointment with the doctor as Frank would want to know why, so I freshen up and call a cab. But it doesn't come quick enough and I hear the pounding of footsteps heading towards the bedroom.

"Autum, are you upstairs?"

I don't answer as I grab my bag and head for the door. With any luck the cab should be coming up the drive right now. *If only...* all I could think of is how Rosetta has put me right in it. *Oh shit...*

Chapter Six

As Frank comes through the door, I speak first to try and catch him off guard.

"Before you say anything, Rosetta's probably made it out to sound worse than it was." I feel quite proud of myself for my quick reply as he catches his breath.

"Rosetta? What's she got to do with this?" *Ok then, not what I expected him to say. Now I've dropped her in it.*

"I thought..." I decide to just give up. I'm not going to win any type of argument now. Let Frank say what he needs to say. Still, I try playing dumb one last time.

"Is something wrong?"

"Wrong? Do you take me for a complete idiot? What happened at lunchtime?"

I will the taxi driver to sound the horn anytime now but nothing happens. I don't know what he knows or how much he knows so I give nothing away.

"I had lunch at..."

"Cut the bullshit Autum. I had a visit this afternoon from a very upset and smelly Isobelle."

"I bet she must have loved that. What did she say?" I go on playing the fool as I bet she failed to mention the fact that Jack pushed me up against a wall and tried to strangle me.

"That she was having lunch and the next thing she knew, you'd poured your drink on her and thrown your food all over her for no reason. She says there were loads of witnesses to back up her story if she decides to take it further."

"That lying bitch! Wait till I see her. I know you won't believe me, but it wasn't like that." I fling down my bag and start to mumble under my breath when I hear the taxi horn. "Great," I say, exiting the room.

"Where are you going?"

"To see the shrink, remember?"

"Doctor," he corrects me.

"Whatever, I've got to go." I hit his shoulder as I walk past.

"Autum..." I turn around.

"WHAT?"

"I'm coming with you and you can tell me what happened in the car. I'll get rid of the taxi and drive you there."

When Isobelle got home after work, Jack asked her if she had said exactly what he had told her to say to Frank.

"Yes I did, and you should have seen his face." She started to laugh. "I was already crying when I reached reception and the more people I drew in, the more dramatic I got. Then I asked Frank's PA Tracey to let me see him and she refused, so I just burst in anyway, Tracey telling me to stop and that he was busy.

"Frank was on a call and ended it quite abruptly. He asked what the hell was going on. Tracey started to say something but he said it was ok and to shut the door behind her. I laid on the waterworks until he actually put his arm around me and told me to sit down.

"I said that I was having lunch and when I looked up, Autum was standing in front of me. I asked her if she was ok as I knew that her and Rebecca had had some disagreement and thought she might be upset. Well, you should have seen the look on Frank's face as she obviously had not told him about that. Anyway, I go on to say that even though she doesn't talk to me doesn't mean I still don't care about her."

"Go on," said Jack.

"Then I say she just attacked me, first with her drink, and then throwing her food in my face when I stood up. I told him that what shocked me the most was that she'd smiled at me, then slapped me in the face and walked out."

"Good girl," said Jack, laughing and giving Isobelle a kiss.

"Did I do well?"

"Better than well." He let out a haughty laugh.

We've almost got to Dr Hillard's when Frank looks at me, concerned.

"So what you're saying in a nutshell is that she wanted to become your friend and you not only throw your drink and food at her but slap her in the face for good measure?" Frank's tone of voice made it sound even worse.

"Something like that. But she was asking for it. She was teasing me and I flipped."

"You can't go around attacking people - you know that don't you? Regardless of whether she deserved it or not, how can you move on if you still let her get to you like that?" He pauses for a second. "Are you sure there is nothing else that I need to know?" He glances at me to gauge my response.

"No, nothing else." But as we reach Dr Hillard's, I hear him take in a deep breath and sigh. We're a few minutes early so stay in the car.

"If you need me..." he says and he gently slips his hand into mine. The warmth sets my heart racing. Whatever I do, he's always there: my rock and my angel, all in one.

I kiss him before I exit the car and get butterflies in my stomach. I turn round and wave to Frank; he waves back.

At reception, an old lady looks up and asks for my name.

"Mrs Howard."

"Take a seat and I will let him know you've arrived." I sit down.

What a blooming day, I think to myself, and now I'll have some goody two-shoes trying to explore my inner thoughts and tell me that I am losing it. But guess what, I can save him the bother and tell him that myself. This meeting should last around five minutes then.

"Mrs Howard?" I snap out of it.

"Uh, yes?"

"You can go in now. Second door on your right."

"Thank you." I start to feel sick. I knock on the door.

"Enter." I walk in.

Dr Hillard looked nothing like the way I had pictured him in my mind. He was quite tall, with a full head of hair and a slim build. He shook my hand firmly and told me to sit down, not on the sofa just yet but on another chair. A doctor he was not; a shrink he definitely was. The room was perfectly white, with minimal furnishings other than a long black leather sofa, if you could call it that. It would fit anybody and allow them to totally relax, which is what it was all about: for you to free up you mind and pour out your troubles.

"So, Mrs Howard..."

"Please, call me Autum."

"Ok, Autum." He writes it down on his pad. "This session is for you. You can be as open and honest as you want to be. I may ask you questions from time to time so that I can make recommendations or get a better understanding of what may be troubling you."

His voice has already started to make me relax and I just want to let it all out. I'm not yet ready for that though.

"Ok then, let's get you to feel more relaxed. I know you must be feeling a little apprehensive but there is nothing to worry about. Just lie back, take in a few deep breaths and close your eyes."

I do as I'm told, closing my eyes and breathing in. I'm shocked at how relaxing this damn sofa is. *I could do with one of these at home.* Then he starts to talk.

"Breathe in… then out, in…. then out. Now tell me, Autum, about your childhood." I feel myself smiling as I begin to talk, happy memories bursting in my mind.

As Frank waited in the car, he went over what Isobelle had said to him in his office. He didn't understand why Autum hadn't told him about her falling out with Rebecca and that worried him immensely. What had they fallen out about?

The ball was in two days time but he couldn't look forward to it until this matter had been resolved. Rebecca and Julian were attending and he didn't want there to be any animosity and tension between the girls, making it awkward for both himself and Julian in the process. He racked his brain for a solution and jumped when his phone went off. It was Rosetta.

"Will you be dining out this evening, Mr Howard?"

"No Rosetta, thank you for asking. We may be home late but could you still prepare something for us?"

"Of course, you don't need to ask, have a good evening." Rosetta was about to hang up. Frank hesitated.

"What happened when my wife came home today?" The silence was deafening. "Rosetta, are you still there?"

"Mr Howard, you have been very good to me but I think you really need to ask Mrs Howard why she looked the way she did."

"What do you mean? Look the way she did? What are you trying to tell me? Please Rosetta, I need to know." She paused and spoke rapidly in Spanish before answering.

"She looked like... She looked as if she had been attacked. She begged me not to tell you, kept crying, but said she would be ok. Please, Mr Howard, I promised her...." And with that, she fell silent.

"I won't let on, thank you." He hung up the phone.

Attacked. But by whom? Rebecca? No way, although Isobelle did say that they had a falling out. But over what?

The questions came readily, but no answers, so Frank did the next best thing and decided to ring Rebecca.

Rebecca had just returned from the office and kicked off her shoes when her mobile rang. She paused for a second when Frank's name flashed on her screen. She couldn't think why he was calling her; maybe he needed something from the office. She answered the call.

"Hi Rebecca," said Frank, slightly croakily.

"Are you ok, Frank? Not coming down with a cold, are you?"

"I need to know why you and Autum had a falling out."

"Is that what she told you?" Frank was silent for a second, enough to tell Rebecca that he was fishing for some answers.

"Isobelle told me."

"What? I don't understand, how did she know?"

"So you *have* had a falling out then."

He'd got her but Rebecca still couldn't understand where Isobelle fitted into this.

"We just had a girlie tiff, that's all."

"Enough to attack her?"

"What? Autum has been attacked? Oh good God, Frank, you should know me better than that. I can't believe you would think I would do something like that to anyone, let alone Autum."

"So you know nothing of what happened today then."

"No, I'm sorry. Is she ok?"

"She's fine, but you still won't tell me what your 'tiff' was about." His voice was sterner this time.

"Like I said, Frank, it really was nothing. I'll call her later and will you tell her for me..." Rebecca fell silent. It was a while before Frank replied.

"She'll be glad to hear from you." He hung up.

An hour had passed and I was sitting up talking to Dr Hillard.

"You did very well today. How have you found it?"

"It wasn't what I was expecting. Well, I didn't know what I was expecting really but I do feel much more relaxed now. So what happens next?"

"I would suggest another appointment in two weeks' time. These sessions are to get you to open up your mind but it takes time. We will both know when that time is but for now, well done." We shook hands and I left the room.

I booked in my next appointment and felt like I was walking on air. The session had gone great and it had been nice to remember my childhood. *Oh happy days.* I smiled at Frank as I walked back to the car, happy that he had recommended I do this. He didn't smile back. Confused at what could have happened since I had last seen him just over an hour before, I felt my uneasiness creeping back and my tension building. *So much for relaxation, knew it was too good to be true.* I opened the car door and got in.

"Is everything ok?" Frank looked at me as if I were his worst enemy, someone that had betrayed him. He looked lost. He tried to put on a smile and started the engine. Now I was worried.

"My session went well" I said as he drove off, again trying to break the ice. Frank stared straight ahead and mumbled,

"Glad it went well." No more was said.

We continued to drive in silence until fifteen minutes later when he pulled into a local pub. He got out and I followed, shocked that he held my hand as we went inside.

"Are you hungry?" His voice was low and sad but I struggled to understand why.

"Not really, but can I have a white wine please?" I went to find us a private corner.

Frank joined me shortly afterwards with his glass of coke and a ticket, which I gathered meant he'd ordered some food.

"Are we good, Frank?" I needed to start this conversation off.

"I need to ask you a question and would like you to *think* about your answer."

I racked my brain to think what might be troubling him but came up blank.

"Why did you and Rebecca fall out?"

What the hell could I say? Wasn't expecting that. Had he spoken to her in the car? I just needed time to think but if I took too long he would know I was trying to think up an excuse. This seemed serious and I had no get out of jail free card. He was testing me and I was not going to fail. If he left me after this, at least it would be because I had chosen to tell him the truth. I braced myself for a possible showdown, relieved that we were at least in public. I began.

"When I left work late that night and was waiting for a taxi outside, I, err, I bumped into Jack." I waited for a response... none... but his eyebrow shifted as he sipped his drink.

"I was shocked, I think, as he'd taken me by surprise. He said "Hi" and I replied, then he asked me if we liked his gift and I said yes. Then my taxi arrived and I got in it; that's all."

"If that's all that happened, why has Rebecca got the hump with you?"

I swallowed hard. The next bit was going to be hard for me to say.

"She was mad for different reasons, I think. Possibly she was shocked that I even spoke to him after everything that had happened, but it was just an instant reaction. And maybe it brought up memories she didn't want. We were having lunch at the time and she got up and left. She hasn't spoken to me since. I was giving her time to calm down.

"You probably won't understand when I say this, but that night, for the first time, I didn't feel threatened by him. He looked and sounded like the old Jack that I knew and lov..." I stopped myself before the whole word came out but I think Frank knew what I was going to say.

"Do you still love him?" Frank looked me straight in the eye. I took his hand.

"I love you Frank. Never doubt that. When he was there I felt hypnotised. Why I don't know but I did and I'm not proud of that. But whatever feelings I had for him disappeared months ago. I don't look at him or think of him that way. I hope you know that."

We both fell silent again while Frank ate his salmon risotto. My heart was working overtime and I took this timeout to let it go back to normal.

"By the way, Rebecca said she will call you later," said Frank and carried on eating.

So he had spoken to Rebecca. Had her version matched up with mine? I presumed so unless he was preparing for round two at home.

By the time we got home it was after eight at night. Rosetta smiled at me but gave me *that look*. We all know that you're in trouble when you get *that look* from an adult. When Frank went into his study, I apologised to Rosetta for the way I had behaved when I came home earlier. I told her that I should never have put her in that position.

"As long as you and Mr Howard are fine, that's all I need to know."

I joined her in the kitchen to get something to eat as I hadn't had the stomach to finish my meal earlier. I tried to make a light hearted joke of it all in my head.

Later, I retired to my room, took a quick shower and relaxed on the bed... My phone rings: *Rebecca*. I say "Hi" and she replies,

"Frank told me that you were attacked today. Are you ok?"

So that's what he thought? But where did he get that idea from? Then I remembered the state I'd come home in. He had talked to Rosetta.

"I wasn't attacked, I just had a run-in with Isobelle at lunchtime. I threw my food and drink at her and I slapped her."

"It must have been *some* run-in for you to do that. I feel bad that you had to deal with that by yourself."

"Don't worry, I'm fine." I talk about my visit to the Doctor to change the subject.

Frank enters the room to see me on the phone and I mouth that it's Rebecca. I laugh and he kisses me on the cheek and heads for the shower.

CHAPTER SEVEN

It is now Friday and both Frank and I are working from home. Frank is making loads of calls regarding the charity ball tomorrow and I am finalising the flowers, confirming guest speakers, organising the champagne reception... the list goes on.

I have spoken to Rebecca a few times today and still have some reports to hand in by Monday. My adrenaline from the amount of work makes the day go by quickly. I speak to the girls for a quick catch up and tell them that I cannot wait for tomorrow and that it's a shame that they can't make it: at two hundred and fifty pounds, the ball tickets had a hefty price, but well worth it for the causes it would benefit.

I take a break and see how Frank is getting on and whether he needs me to do anything else. I walk in and he's slouched back on his chair, burnt out. He looks so sexy in his casual trousers and polo shirt. I know he obviously needed a rest but would he let *me* rest? I don't think so. A smile lights up my face as I remember some good times in this room. I go over to kiss the top of his forehead, taking in his scent. He struggles to open his eyes. "Sleepy babes," I say as he sits upright.

"Just a cat nap, better for seeing you here." He swirls round and sweeps me onto his lap. I giggle and give him a full on kiss, which *should* only last seconds. But the more we kiss, the more aroused we both get, the deeper our tongues go. All I can think about is having sex in this room again and again. I lift up my skirt as I straddle him, Frank parting my legs to accommodate his bulging pants, his hands gliding through my hair getting a better grip. He moves up and down, rubbing me slightly..

"I thought you were tired?" I whisper in his ear, my nose brushing down his cheek towards his lips.

"Just need a pick me up," he laughs and I laugh too.

I feel his hands under my vest top, the heat adding to the pleasure I was already feeling.

"No bra, Mrs Howard?" A smile lights up his face.

My cheeks heat as my nipples harden, waiting for him to touch them, suck them, taken them in his mouth. He removes my top by slow torture and throws it on the floor.

"So hard, yet so demanding," he says, as he flicks each one with his tongue in quick succession. He slows down to circle them, looking at me before sucking my breast, never severing eye contact. I feel the heat go through me, hitting my chest first, moving down my spine, my inner thighs melting to the touch, before it heads to my toes and back round my body over and over again.

I remove his polo shirt and lean into him, my chest squashing against his. He lifts my skirt even higher and slides his fingers into my panties.

"You're dripping." He pulls his fingers out and tastes them. "Hmm, this is a good year." I give him a playful slap and he returns that smile again, before sliding his fingers back in.

"I'm going to fuck you in this chair, Mrs Howard, before I put you on the table." I love how he calls my name. His hot breath sweeps past my ear and my body responds, awaiting his next move. I moan with the pleasure that I'm getting and for what's in store for me, the wetness even greater than before. He removes his fingers and a sweep of coldness passes by. I hold my breath waiting for his fingers to return, my clit throbbing for more contact.

"Stand up," he says and I do what I'm told, pulling down my skirt at the same time. Why? To look more dignified. *Well that's what I try to convince myself anyway.*

"Take off your panties." I obey slipping out of them slowly but seductively, swaying from side to side. As they hit the floor, I kick them away.

Frank tells me to sit down and kneels in front of me. Then, with a sudden jerk, he yanks me towards him, heightening my sex to a new level. My legs thrown over his shoulders and his fingers back inside of me, I lean back into the chair, drugged by it all. I feel his tongue flicking my clit and I struggle to focus.

"Look at me," he says and I watch him. I feel weak as his tongue works in harmony with his fingers, I feel myself coming and my moans get louder and louder until I explode. I hold the chair tight, buckling after my orgasm, while Frank watches me, continuing to pump his fingers.

"Stand," he says, but I can hardly get up. My knees are on the verge of giving in. He clears a space on his desk and pulls down his trousers and boxers, his cock springing free and ready for action.

"Look at me." Again I do and his cock enters me a split second later, taking my breath away. His thrusts are full of passion but hard like a battering ram, his length, his width and the hardness taking no prisoners. He pumps harder and harder, his fullness sending pleasure and pain throughout my whole body. I try to grip the desk but my hands keep sliding to the side. He lifts me off, turns me around and enters me from behind all in the blink of an eye. I hold on for dear life, my breasts flapping up and down with the force. He spreads my legs even further and holds onto my waist for support as he relentlessly plunges deeper, his balls giving my clit a good old fashion beating. His breathing changes and I can feel him swelling even more inside me. He makes a few noises before he releases everything he has inside me, letting out his own guttural cry. It takes some time for Frank to calm down and get his body under control. As for me, well, I won't be running any marathons soon. The only thing I could do with now is an ambulance. There is one thing that I would like to say though and that is that *everyone needs a study.*

We both straighten back the study to how it was *before* I came in and I leave Frank to continue working now he's had his pick me up.

I go into the kitchen to get a light snack that Rosetta has left for me and Frank, still struggling to gain full use of my body and legs. My clit is throbbing uncontrollably and the rest of me is aching but that makes it more enjoyable and memorable.

I need a shower and as I head towards the stairs, Frank is just ahead of me, climbing two steps at a time. *How the hell has he still got energy to do that?* I hold onto the hand rail as if I am climbing the Great Wall of China and take them one by one at the slowest pace my body can handle. As I reach the bedroom, Frank is already in the shower. I decide it's too dangerous to go in there as I think he is now running on Duracell batteries. I'll wait until he is *out* before I go *in.*

I check my phone to see if I have missed any messages, which I have: two with no number and one from Rebecca. Frank starts to sing and I just shake my head. *Incredible...*

I go to put my phone down and it rings – *no number* – but I answer it anyway, probably someone asking me to update to the latest phone package deal.

"Hello?"

"I'm so sorry about yesterday. Please forgive me. I could never hurt you again." Then the line goes dead.

No fucking way could he have got my number. No way. I hold the phone in front of me as if *that* is going to give me answers. Will he never give up? *Mind games* that's all he's doing, but I can't shake the bloody phone call out of my mind. Why would he need my forgiveness? What is he playing at? *Don't let him get to you. Happy thoughts, remember?*

I feel cold goose bumps on my skin. I can't tell Frank because that will just open up a hornet's nest and now I can't tell Rebecca either. It's as if he knows whenever I'm having fun and always wants to spoil the party. Well guess what Jack, once bitten, twice shy. I lay the phone on the bed and decide to join Mr Duracell in the bathroom.

I'd cleared most of my important emails by late afternoon but the calls kept coming regarding the ball. I felt like a secretary going backward and forward confirming details with Frank. He once caught me jumping when my phone went off but I just pretended that I was daydreaming. It was after nine before we finally called it a day and ate. God, this was worse than being at work. I was totally shattered and could not wait to go to bed. I told Frank to call it a night but workaholic that he is, I knew it would be early morning before I would feel my heat source next to me. By the time I hit the bed I was out for the count. Then my mind was woken up by a dream...

Isobelle was crying, like I give a damn, but she seemed to be consoling me? I couldn't see myself or understood the meaning of what she was doing, but I was screaming at her for some reason, which felt more like it.

"Get away from me, bitch." That's all I remember saying. She kept repeating that she was sorry but I couldn't work out what for.

I felt myself turning in bed, trying to look around at where I was. A log cabin? How weird, beautiful but eerie at the same time, surrounded by trees and a lake. It was broad daylight and you could just about hear the water running by. The cabin was big and fully furnished with all the mod cons.

There were windows on every side from floor to ceiling, letting in light. It felt so peaceful.

I heard footsteps and doors shutting. Isobelle looked towards where the noise was coming from as Jack entered the room. He gave her a look and she left, leaving me with him. I glanced up at him before I went on the attack.

Then I woke up. My first instinct was to analyse it but I decided not to. Nothing a dream could do or say would make me feel like I did all those months ago. I felt better: I wasn't letting them take over my life and the dreams I had had so far were so random they weren't even worth a second thought. I turned to find the bed still empty, the time: two in the morning. I turned over and went back to sleep.

Frank was working late downstairs when he got a call. He smiled, thinking it might be his sexy wife calling him to bed, telling him that she was naked, wet and waiting for him to come upstairs so that she could suck his cock. He let the thought pass, the smile now quickly removed from his face. It wasn't a number he recognised but the day he'd had, it didn't matter. Everyone who was anyone was ringing for last minute invites to the ball. Word had been spreading and it was going to be the place to be. He'd laughed with his friends, colleagues and business associates, and thought again about the time he had with Autum, he'd made some hard business decisions that day but nothing could have prepared him for the call he was about to receive. It was Jack.

"How did you get this number?" Frank said, his tone sharp and to the point.

"We have more important things to discuss than how I got your number, don't you think?" He could tell Jack was smirking, felt it go through him as he spoke.

"I don't know what you're on about."

"Autum." Frank felt the evil in his voice, the threat in his tone.

"You mean my wife." Frank could hear Jack's breathing getting heavy.

"I think you mean MINE." Jack hung up the phone. It took Frank a few seconds to digest the conversation before he threw his phone down and ran upstairs like a madman. He expected Autum to be gone but she was stirring in her sleep safely in her bed. Frank looked around and checked all the windows, cupboards and doors in the room. He realised he was getting paranoid, yet he still couldn't settle until he had checked the entire house.

He knew the incident had shaken him up and he was shocked with himself that it had. Then he remembered how it must have felt for Autum, alone with a madman. Why she dropped those charges…he couldn't understand.

Jack was sending out a warning, not to Autum but to Frank. He wanted to take Frank on. Frank would do whatever it took to keep Autum safe. But Jack was upping his game and Frank knew the stakes were going to be high.

Frank pulled out some old contacts of his and made a few phone calls. It was two in the morning and Frank apologised to his friends for the late hour and explained the urgency of the call. He chatted with the first friend for twenty minutes, then dialled another number and so on. Once he was happy that things were in place, he went to bed just before three.

I woke up early and excited: today was the day of the ball. I jumped on Frank and told him to wake up as I kissed him on the cheek. Little did I know that Frank was already awake. He greeted me with a kiss then rolled me over so that I was under him.

"I love you. You know that don't you?" he said, spreading my legs.

"I love you too, with all my heart," I replied as he slid down my body planting kisses all over. I started to fidget as my body warmed up, feeling his lips travelling down my neck, his tongue slowly licking me, and his lips curving around my nipple, soft and warm. His hands slid down and removed my bottoms as I guided my hand through his hair. I lifted my hips as I felt his hot breath between my legs, wanting him to make contact.

"I can't lose you," he said. As his tongue made contact, I moaned and widened my legs even more, lost in his shaky breath.

"You never will," I replied, my voice but a whisper. He rose up and looked me in the eye, his eyes looking lost and torn.

"Fuck me, Frank, I need to feel you inside me." He entered me slowly, savouring our time together, the thickness feeling so good inside. The slower his body moved, the more pressure inside, the better it felt. Even though the feeling was good, I wanted Frank to enjoy what I was enjoying and I rolled him over so that I could see him from above, the man I love beneath me sending shock waves up my body. I grinded on him as he grabbed my breast lifting himself into me. As I made love to him, I watched his face light up, as we both go over the edge and come together. *Nothing could spoil this beautiful moment*, I say to myself, *Nothing*.

CHAPTER EIGHT

Frank puts his tuxedo on, fixes his hair and tops up his aftershave.

"Autum, hurry up, we need to get there early." Panic in his voice.

I've hidden my dress for so long and now, at last, I walk into the bedroom to see if Frank likes it.

"You like?" I say, swirling round, the dress hugging my figure. I've never really seen his face make an expression like that before so I must assume that I look ok!

"You look amazing," he says, finally closing his mouth, "You never stop surprising me. And by the way, you're not leaving my sight in that dress." He heads towards me and gives me a hug.

"Thank you," I say, "Got to look good next to my husband, now don't I?"

"Autum, I need to tell you something."

Frank never stutters but for some reason he does now. I felt it this morning but shrugged it off.

"Is something wrong, Frank?" I say, concerned, and hold onto his arm.

"I have hired a bodyguard for you today, just in case. You know, just in case anything happens."

"Has something happened that you're not telling me about?" My heart starts to race. Did he find out about me being attacked? "Frank, you're scaring me." I feel myself getting emotional.

"Autum, don't. Please. I just want to make sure nothing happens. I don't want to lose you. Now let's go, I don't want us to be late." He wipes a tear from my eye.

Throughout the journey, Frank keeps fidgeting and I put it down to nerves. He may do these charity balls on a regular basis but he always gets nerves before he arrives, his brain working overtime checking that there will be no catering mishaps or worrying in case the microphones aren't working or they run out of drinks for the champagne reception. I put my hand on his knee for reassurance and give him a loving smile. *Stop worrying, Frank, it will fine.*

We pull up outside of the hotel along with a stream of cars turning up like a production line. I'm greeted by what can only be described as a hulk, his muscles are so big there's no way he could be any less discrete!

Frank does all the introductions as we enter the building, before we get surrounded by guests, shaking Frank's hand and giving him pats on the back or bombarding me with "That dress is amazing!"'s and kisses on the cheek. I hear someone call my name amongst the hoards of people and spot Rebecca and Julian heading my way. What a relief. I say to Mr Hulk that I will be fine now and that he doesn't need to stay with me but all he says is,

"I was given strict order not to let you out of my sight." *This is going to be a bundle of laughs,* I think to myself.

"What's with the bodyguard?" says Julian.

"I have no idea," I reply

"Has something happened?" Rebecca asks.

"That's what I'm going to find out!" And with that we headed for the main hall and took our seats. There were a few spaces with "Reserved" written on them but I couldn't work out who they were for: the hulk took up a space next to me, but there were still two places left. Then as more people started sitting at their allotted tables, all I could here was "Excuse me... Sorry! Thanks..." and a smile came to my face. Emily and Dionne were heading my way.

"We wanted to surprise you and offer support for a fantastic charity."

I was choked. I think everything had just started to build up and the silliest things were now setting me off, now I understood who would be sitting at those reserved places.

"Are you ok?" they all seemed to say in unison.

"Better for seeing all my friends." Then we all broke out into chatter as poor Julian said he was leaving to find Frank.

The evening was going well and our table was filled with food and bucket after bucket of wines and champagne, but every time I needed to go to the ladies', the hulk was not far behind.

"Really?" I said, looking at him, but all he did was give that stern look back.

I didn't bother Frank as he was so busy. I hardly had five minutes with him at the table. He just kissed me on the cheek and I felt the reassurance of his hand slip up my thigh before he was off again meeting someone. At least he looked a lot more relaxed.

Before we knew it, all five courses had been demolished and it was time for some dancing. Rebecca was led to the floor by Julian, then Frank followed suit. As for the hulk? He may not have been on the dance floor but by God his eyes were scanning everywhere.

"Are we expecting company?" I asked Frank as he twirled me round.

"There's a lot of people here; anything could happen." He gripped my waist more tightly.

"Am I in some sort of danger, Frank?" He stopped in the middle of our dance and looked at me.

"Just want my gorgeous wife to be safe that's all" he kisses my check and we continue our dance.

After the third dance, he took a breather and I did the same, needing to go to the bar for a stronger drink. I fought through the crowd and waited with the queue of people all trying to get a drink. Then the smell hit me, Issey Miyake. No other man could carry that scent the way Jack does. Now I understood why Frank had hired the hulk.

I felt a hand slide across my back but I did not turn round, just took a deep breath before I exhaled. I glanced around quickly then looked for my bodyguard just in case I freaked out. He sensed it and in a blink of an eye I was escorted out and into the hallway.

"He's here." That's all I said before the hulk was talking into his earpiece. But to whom? I have no idea.

"Are you alright?" His voice was deep but gentle, his big hands soft on my shoulder.

"Yes. Can I go now, please?" I was shaky and knew Jack had got the upper hand.

Why was he even here? He was taking a risk even by his standards. Did Frank know he was coming?

I felt like I was going to throw up and headed for the bathroom to freshen up. As I take a swig of water, I hear:

"You really do look amazing..." I pause for a moment before I realise that my second worse nightmare is here, Isobelle.

"What are you doing here, Isobelle? You have no right to be here."

"I've paid my money like everybody else here tonight. Why shouldn't we be here?" That's the icing on the cake: "we".

"You're here with Jack?"

"Who else," she says, topping up her lipstick in the mirror, "Autum, please stop treating me like this. I see you had no problems inviting Emily and Dionne."

"I can't do this right now," I say and go to leave.

"I won't give up trying." She tries to grab hold of my arm.

I scream at the contact, probably because I'm not expecting it and because I'm not in a good place. Before the scream has even settled, the hulk bursts through the door. He pushes Isobelle out of the way before escorting me out the bathroom without a second glance.

I didn't want to leave without saying goodbye to my friends but I had no choice. I was taken to a car already waiting in the parking lot with another bodyguard holding open the door. I was quickly put inside as he went round to the front passenger side and off the car drove.

I ran inside and straight upstairs. I didn't ring Frank, as I knew they must have informed him of what had happened. My phone rang shortly afterwards. I answered it.

"You looked so divine tonight, I *had* to touch you."

"So I was right. It was you, Jack. When will you learn? You will never have me. Ever."

"I should have fought harder for you."

"I still wouldn't have you back, Jack. Whatever we had has gone, and the sooner you realise that the better."

"Don't say that Autum. Please, I love you and always will. Frank is the problem but not for much longer..." Before I could reply he hung up.

I panicked and rang Frank several times but it went to voicemail. I ran back downstairs, my dress nearly killing me as I almost missed a step in my heels. I headed outside to drive the car but was shocked to see the hulk outside my house. I paused, more out of confusion, before I told him to drive me back to the ball.

It took forty-five minutes to arrive back at the ball and it was as if I'd never left. I worked my way back through the crowd to find Frank talking to some colleagues. I slipped my hand around his waist to get his attention and he cut the conversation short. He looked up at the hulk but I drew his face to me.

"I asked him to bring me back. I needed to make sure you were ok."

"Why didn't you tell me that Jack and Isobelle were here?" He held my waist as he led me away from the crowd, followed by our friend.

"I wasn't sure he was coming, but after the phone call..."

"What phone call? When did you speak to him?" He hesitated before he responded. "Jack rang me late last night when you were sleeping. He said that you were his and hung up. I thought he was in the house and for a split second I panicked and thought he was trying to take you from me. I wasn't going to take any chances."

"So you hired the bodyguards?"

"Yes."

"Do you know why I came back? Because he rang me too, said that *you* were the problem but 'not for much longer'. I'm scared Frank, what can we do?" He kissed me gently. "Stay with the girls, Jack and Isobelle have been escorted discretely off the premises and the night is drawing to a close. We can talk more when we get home." With that, he blended back into the crowd, his business face back on and working his audience.

Emily and Dionne both approached me. "Where have you been? We were looking all over for you."

"I was here, just mingling and being the good host. Sorry didn't mean for you all to worry." *I was praying that the shame I felt was not showing on my face.*

"I'm not sure we should tell you but..."

"No need. I saw them both."

"And you're ok with that?"

"Yep, I've moved on." And I mumbled to myself, "It's a shame they haven't."

I pulled the girls onto the dance floor so that we could end the night on a high. It was very hard to really get down and boogie when we all were wearing figure hugging gowns but hey, it was fun trying. As the hours passed, the crowds started to disperse until the girls, Rebecca and Julian, were saying goodbye. I felt the emptiness as I was alone with the hulk waiting for Frank to join me. I tried to build up conversation but he must have been on a "no talking unless I'm under attack" contract, which made the wait even longer.

Once we are back home, Frank and I decide to sit down and talk about the events of the day. I slip out of my dress into something more comfortable and Frank does the same as we sit up in bed to talk.

"He's after you?" says Frank.

"I know and it scares me. Can't we report it to the police?"

"Not much to go on. Have no proof he has contacted us. It will be his word against ours."

I cuddle Frank to feel more secure.

"I should have ended this when I had the chance," I mumble under my breath.

"What's done is done," says Frank and ends the conversation there.

Sleeping is hell that night as I go through what Jack said on the phone, "Frank is the problem... Please forgive me... I would never hurt you again and I love you." This was my problem but now Frank has been dragged into my mess yet again. I turn to look at him sleeping peacefully, unaware of what could possibly lie ahead. I yawn as I slowly drift off to sleep.

When Frank woke, he needed to relax so he contacted his friends to play a round of golf. I decided that this was a good time to settle things once and for all. I love Frank too much to ever put him in danger. I headed down to his study and ran my hand along the desk, a smile lighting up my tormented face. I stop and scan the room and remember the time Frank caught me in his shirt and pinned me to the floor. I focus my eyes on the spot. His chair is the next thing I look at before I take a seat in it. It is soft, comfortable and moulded to Frank's body. I close my eyes and think of the fun we have had before a pain hits my chest. *You're doing the right thing and you know it.*

I take a piece of paper and start to write.

My darling Frank,

This is the hardest thing I have ever had to do for the man I love.

When we met, I knew you were the one for me from our first kiss, the taste of champagne and strawberries still fresh in my mind.

You melted my heart, mind and soul. Even though it was never meant to be, you were always there. So many times you turned out to be my knight in shining armour and I wondered what I did to deserve such a loving man, a man who ended up with so much baggage but never gave up fighting for the woman he confessed to loving. Now I am returning the favour.

It is because I love you so much that I cannot bear the thought of anyone ever hurting you to get to me, especially someone like Jack. I'm not worth it, and if it means me not being around you to keep you safe, then that is the price I am wiling to pay.

Never think I don't love you... I do.

I feel empty at the loss I now feel, knowing I will never see you again.

Don't look for me, Frank, because you won't find me. Send Rebecca and Rosetta my love.

Please forgive me, Frank, I really wanted to make you proud of me. I wanted this to work but I just keep failing.

Bye Frank
I Love You
Autum xx

By the time I've finished writing, the tears are flowing freely down my face. I know it is the right thing to do and feel no regret, so why is my heart in so much pain?

I pick up the letter and put it in an envelope marked "Frank". As I leave the study, I pick up the keys to the lodge from one of his cabinets. Frank only uses it occasionally and wouldn't even think of looking for me there.

As I leave the study, I take my last look around the place I call home, pick up my suitcase and bags, leave my keys and walk out the door, sobbing with every step. *Goodbye Frank...* I headed for the car.

CHAPTER NINE

Frank arrived home three hours later, laughing his head off at beating his friends on the golf course. He hadn't played for some time but obviously had not lost his touch at the game, or at the jokes he kept playing in the bar afterwards.

He had brought the biggest bouquet of flowers home for his wife and her favourite champagne. He wanted to talk about them trying for a baby. He didn't care about the Birmingham office anymore, only Autum. She was the best thing that could have happened to him. It was only when he'd heard his mates talking about their own children that he'd decided he did not want to wait any longer.

He ran upstairs and took a shower, still in a jolly mood. He then changed into something light and went to his study. He hadn't even noticed how quiet the house was or the fact that his other car was missing from the drive. He sat in his chair, swivelled it towards his desk, then froze. In front of him was the envelope with his name on it. He knew it was from Autum, could smell traces of her perfume on the envelope. His body slouched as he sat back in his chair. He opened the envelope with shaky hands and started to read the letter. All he read was "My darling Frank" and he fell apart. He pulled himself together enough to continue reading until he finished and collapsed over his desk, crying uncontrollably. "Autum!" he shouted, as if she would walk through the door towards him half naked. He was getting pains in his chest and thought he was having a heart attack. His focus was blurred as he tried to think. He ran back upstairs and checked the rooms. Cupboard after cupboard were empty; she had taken as much as she could possibly carry, leaving only a few clothes and shoes. He took out his phone and dialled her number and heard her phone ringing – it was on the dresser. He ran back downstairs and cried out for Rosetta.

"Where is she?" He shook her harder than he intended to.

"Who, Mr Howard?"

"My wife! Where is she? She must have said something to you."

"I don't know, Mr Howard. I didn't even hear her leave. Is something wrong?" He dialled Rebecca's number and headed back to the study.

"She's left me," were the first words that Rebecca heard from a sobbing Frank.

"Calm down, Frank. You're not making sense."

"She's gone, Rebecca. She's gone."

"But how? Why? I don't understand, I thought everything was fine between you two?"

"Help me find her. Please. I love her. I'm nothing without her, Rebecca, nothing." Frank continued to cry down the phone; Rebecca told him she would be round with Julian and for him to remain calm.

When they arrived, Frank was still crying, eyes red and puffy. All Rebecca could do was watch him come to her and cry.

"She's left me this," he said, showing them the letter, "I have to find her, before *he does*. She's scared and thought she would be protecting me but she's the one that needs protecting." He continued to cry.

They all sat down in Frank's study going through the events leading up to that day. Rebecca listed all the places that she remembered Autum saying she liked and the places she wanted to visit, even though she had not known her long enough to build up an extensive list. Julian couldn't help much so could only offer support to Frank.

Frank's phone rang shortly afterwards and he nearly stumbled trying to answer it.

"Oh my God, Autum. Where are you?" was the first thing that came out of his mouth.

"I'm fine, Frank. Just wanted you to know that I'm ok."

"Come home, please. We can sort this out together. Just tell me where you are." He continued to cry.

"Don't, Frank. I'm doing this for you."

"He can harm you if we're apart. You're playing right into his hands!"

"Goodbye, Frank."

"Autum! Autum!" The line went dead.

Rebecca gave Frank another hug as he went into meltdown.

Rosetta came in, offering refreshments.

"It may not be of any help, Mr Howard, but at least she has taken the car."

"The car! That's right, it has a tracker in it. Oh, thanks Rosetta." He grabbed her and planted a kiss on her cheek.

Rosetta just tutted as she walked out of the room.

"Frank." Rebecca brought him back to his senses. "Give her some time. If you rush in there and find her she may resent you for it. Let her handle this in her own time. She will come round."

"And if she doesn't?"

"She will. You know her, Frank. You both belong together, not apart. You need a plan for work. Just make sure that you act like nothing is out of the ordinary. Nobody needs to know she's missing."

"I can't."

"Yes you can. As far as work is concerned, she is visiting a sick relative and unsure of how long she may be off."

"I miss her."

"I know you do, but you need to be strong for both of you. Will you be ok?" Frank nodded. "If you need anything, no matter the time, call one of us, you hear?" He nodded again.

I've just arrived at the lodge and settled in. I unload all my bags from the car, take them downstairs and pack them away using all of the wardrobe spaces. I relax and take a long soak in the bath thinking to myself, *did I do the right thing?* It broke my heart when I heard Frank on the phone. He was so distraught, so tearful, all because of me. I needed time to think and couldn't do it at home. I bought myself a cheap mobile phone in case I needed to use one. I needed to make that call to re-assure him that I was safe but now, I don't know whether I made the right choice or made things worse. At least he knows I'm ok.

I slip out, wrap myself up in a thick robe and head upstairs to the kitchen to reheat the takeout food I bought on the way down.

I call my mum and dad in case they call home and tell them that I will be working away on business and that it would be easier if I call them when I am free. I debate whether or not it's a good idea to ring Rebecca but I still need to hear a friend's friendly voice so I call her.

"Hi Rebecca, it's Autum. I just wanted to tell you…"

"I know, I was at Frank's when you phoned." There is silence before I talk back.

"It was for the best."

"The best for whom? You didn't see the state Frank was in. You didn't see a grown man break down in front of his friends. You didn't see him tell me over and over again how much he loves you." I start to cry.

"I was scared, ok? He's after me again. Told me he loved me and that Frank is the problem. I told him it will never happen. He's started to ring me, then I found out he's ringing Frank. I just couldn't take it. He's coming after me and no matter where I am, he's going to find me." I take a long deserved breath – it had all come out in one rushed mouthful.

"You never said things were this bad."

"I don't want him to hurt you or Frank or anyone. If I keep away then he can only come after me, don't you see?"

"And how can we help you then? When you're isolated, alone, and have no one watching your back... Eh? Tell me that."

"Rebecca, you're shouting at me. How do you think I feel? Leaving the man I love in case some nut job of an ex tries to hurt him or you just to get to me. I know I may not have handled this right..."

"You're damn right you haven't. You're being selfish and stupid. All you had to do was press charges but you didn't. You made him believe he was untouchable. YOU'VE created this mess and now we're all walking on eggshells." They're the words I've been dreading to hear. She's right. I dropped the charges because I didn't want the world to know what had happened to me. I was ashamed and I wanted to forget the whole nightmare instead of reliving it and feeling that everyone who looked at me knew what had gone on.

"I didn't realise you still blamed me, Rebecca. I did what I did to deal with the situation and I hate myself for it. I'm so sorry." It's the only thing left I can say. The conversation hurts and I don't want to hear anymore. I end the call.

Monday morning saw Frank go into work but he had cancelled all the meetings that he could and got them re-arranged for the following week. He made a few phone calls about the tracking device in his car and waited for an update. He needed to make sure that Autum was indeed safe and the whereabouts of his car might shed some light.

Rebecca had phoned his internal line to update him on the conversation that her and Autum had had.

"I didn't mean to shout at her, Frank. Just wanted to tell her how much it was affecting you."

"What happened then?" was Frank's reply.

"I kind of blamed her for this whole mess." Rebecca's voice trailed off as she spoke, waiting to gauge Frank's reaction.

"How could you, Rebecca? You're her friend, the only one she's got, and right now she needs you more than ever. Despite whether you think what she did was right or wrong, she needs our support." Frank's voice was broken again and he took in a deep breath. "If she contacts you again, please let me know."

"I will," was all Rebecca said.

Two weeks went by and I did not make any more contact with either Frank or Rebecca. I hired Jose for my stay at the lodge and explained that I was here on business but that Frank would not be joining me. I phoned the police just to find out about the phone calls and make sure they were logged but there was not much that they could do. The fresh air and peace did me a world of good and gave me time to clear my head. I was going to go back home in the next few weeks. I was just praying that my husband would still accept me with open arms.

Frank had received the news he wanted to hear, that the car had been traced to Lincolnshire. His heart skipped a beat to know that she had decided to go to the place where he had first taken her to get better, a place where they talked, laughed and shared there feelings for each other. He needed to be sure she had gone to the lodge so on reaching home he went into his study and into the cabinet to find the keys missing. All he could do was smile and thank the gods he now knew where she was.

He started to pack an overnight bag but then stopped himself. How would she feel if he turned up? Would she run away again? Further this time, somewhere he couldn't find her? Questions but no real answers. He hadn't slept well the last two weeks, his mind filled with awful dreams. This was no way to live. He wasn't going to stop now and he would deal with her reaction to seeing him once he arrived. He finished packing and told Rosetta that he was away for the night and would let her know of any change. Then the door shut and he drove off in his car to get his wife back.

CHAPTER TEN

It was just after nine when Frank's car pulled into the second car parking space next to his lodge. At first he just stared at the car parked beside him, knowing that his wife was just inside those doors, thinking that no one cared enough to find her even though she didn't want to be found. He left his bag in the car and was heading for the door when he heard voices approaching. He backed up a little with shock as mumbled though it was, it was definitely a man's voice he could hear, laughing. *How could she?* He wanted to kick down the door with rage but he was too hurt to even do that. *It's only been two weeks and she's already moved on,* he thought to himself. As the noise grew louder, Frank realised he couldn't move from the door. He needed to confront whatever greeted him when it opened. He heard the latch click and saw the door push open. His heart was pounding because he knew that tonight he was going to have a showdown. When he looked at the man coming out of the door, he took a sigh of relief, both men shocked to see each other. As Jose left the house, the two men exchanged greetings and talked for a few seconds while Frank kept the door open. Then he walked in.

He heard the clink of a glass and thought that she must be pouring a drink, something Frank was in need of himself. His heart was still pounding as he still, even now, was having second thoughts about walking through into the lounge. Every step felt like a knife in the chest. He could hear the music system playing, which made him feel a little calmer. The door was shut to the living room so he decided to knock rather than shock her outright.

"Jose? Is that you? Did you forget something? Come in." Frank thought she sounded jolly. He knew Jose's cooking was her downfall, how much his food excited her. He wanted to chuckle – how had she found out his number? If she let him stay, he would ask her that and so much more.

As he opened the door, her smile dropped and her face turned to shock. She bolted upright from the sofa.

"Frank!" she said, knocking over her glass of wine...

"Shit," I said, referring to two things: Frank being here and the drink all over the floor.

"Leave it," was his reply as I slowly turned to face him, his deep voice sinking inside my body.

"How did you find me?" I tried to hide the way I felt. Deep down, I just wanted to run to him and kiss him. Seeing him in front of me, his sexy body, his puffed eyes and thick stubble got me all worked up.

He stepped closer but I just froze as he slipped off his jacket and loosened his tie.

"How could you leave me the way you did?" I stumbled for words.

"I thought it was for the best. I was thinking of coming back, I swear I was." By the time I finished my sentence, he was in front of me, his hot breath against my face, his breathing erratic. *He's so mad, I can tell.* I put my head in my hands and broke down. Frank's heat radiated around me as he pulled me into his arms.

"I could never hate you, Autum. You're my life, without you I'm nothing." I cried even more.

"I want you to know it broke my heart leaving you. The letter was the hardest thing I have ever done, and I was scared for *you* Frank more than for me. It was one thing Jack hurting me but if he ever hurt you..."

"Shush," he said, pulling the hair away from my face, "We need to talk."

As we both sat on the sofa, I looked at Frank and thought of our life together, how far we had both come and what lay ahead. He's the one that gives me strength and I suddenly realised how weak I was without him.

Jose had cooked a lot of food just for me so I plated some of it up, gave it to Frank and poured him a drink.

"Has Jack made anymore calls?" It was pointless avoiding his name since I was in this situation and it needed addressing.

"He called last week but I just hung up without entertaining him."

"I never thought things would get this bad. I thought his relationship with Isobelle was strong."

"He's obviously putting up a front with the poor cow while he's trying to win you back."

"He hurt me bad, Frank. I can't let him do that to me again."

Frank looked like he wanted to comment on the last statement but realised this was not the right time to do it. He was glad that I was safe and in his arms; I'm sure he wanted to say so many things but he kept quiet.

After Frank had eaten, I cocooned myself into him. As I wrapped my arms around him, I noticed that his heartbeat was fast and his breathing still had not settled. *Is something more bothering him?*

"If I asked you to come back home with me tomorrow, would you?"

That's what was playing on his mind. He was scared that if he asked me, I would say no. I moved my hand across his chest and my suspicion was correct, his heart was beating out of control.

"If you'll still have me," I said trying to calm him.

"Oh God, Autum, I've missed you so much." He smothered my whole face with kisses, the tears filling those beautiful eyes. We watched the night slowly slipping away from us, making love through most of it.

Frank had arranged for Jose to come early in the morning to cook breakfast even though I had arranged for him to start at eight. I stirred in bed and went to cuddle Frank. When I felt the cold space beside me, *he's left me* was the first thing I thought. I shot up and ran through the house calling out his name and crying at the same time. When I reached the lounge, Frank came towards me and asked what was wrong.

"I thought you left me. You were not in bed and I thought you decided that I was too much of a burden and left."

"You're shaking. Come on, sit down."

I still hadn't registered Jose in the room, only Frank's face in front of me; it must have been those familiar smells that jolted me from my thoughts.

"Jose, you're early?" My cheeks started to flush as my attire was a bit revealing.

"Mr Howard wanted me in for six, hope you don't mind."

"No, that's fine," I said, trying to pull what little material I had on closer together.

Frank laughed and nodded. I got up to go back downstairs but not before I feel a sharp slap across my bum. I yelped and turned around to see Frank with a smile and a raised eyebrow.

I wanted to make sure that everything was all right between Frank and me; last night was great but that didn't mean things were back to normal. We wrapped up and headed out onto the trail for walkers to take in the early morning air.

"Sorry I put our marriage at risk," I said, as we walked hand in hand.

"It was never at risk," was Frank's quick reply.

"I contacted the police about the phone calls. Just wanted to know for sure what, if anything, can be done, but you were right – no hard evidence that they can use. But at least it's logged now. Have you spoken to Rebecca?"

"Yes, she told me about your phone call." He knew I hung up on her.

"I can't seem to get anything right, can I?"

"I think you both did what you felt was right at the time and said things that might not have been appropriate looking back. But she will always be there for you, never doubt that."

I smiled up at Frank and we continued our walk.

"Frank, I love it here. Can we try and come down here more often, like every other weekend if you're not too busy?"

"If that's what you want, I will get something arranged." He squeezed my hand.

It was around ten in the morning when we decided it was time to go home.

"What about all of my stuff?"

"We can pick it up another time."

"And the car?"

"Don't worry, that will be taken care of."

He had an answer for everything. And with that, he was starting the engine and we were heading home.

Jack had been busy since the ball and, little did Autum know, he had hired a private investigator to watch her every move and was planning a surprise visit to her *little hideaway*. As he looked at the pictures sent to him of her, alone with bags of clothes, he knew that something must have happened. Could *he* have been the cause of their argument? It must have been quite bad if she had decided to move out. But all Jack could do was smile. He had shots of her leaving the lodge, out shopping and even pictures of the chef. He wanted to know what she was doing throughout the day and expected a report every two hours.

Everything that he had put in place was in order, even the masking tape and rope hidden in the back of his car, but he was in no hurry. He thought that he would have all the time in the world. But now he would have to wait for another opportunity to get back the women he loved. He had found out that Frank had turned up and stayed over and that they had left together. He stared angrily at a picture of them happily getting into the car. *Frank.... always the hero, eh? We'll see about that.* He ripped Frank out of the picture and kissed Autum's face.

There was another big issue heading Jack's way: his father was coming to town and he knew Autum would be the topic of conversation. His father wanted to see her and insisted that on his arrival she would attend lunch, no matter what. He already knew that they had split up and had not taken it well. He also knew about Isobelle but showed no interest in meeting or talking to her. It seemed they both loved Autum in different ways. Maybe if he spoke to her... more ideas kept entering his head. He was happy to meet his father, happier than he ever thought he would be, because now, it would be his father that would reunite him and Autum.

Jack needed to make sure that the office was looking the best it could. He spared no expense, getting in extra cleaners to make sure that there was nothing his father could fault. He re-arranged some meetings to take time out with his father and made sure the reception area was filled invitingly with fresh flowers. Five years and his father decides to visit? He wasn't sure if something else might be on the agenda because his father had given nothing away. Jack didn't even know how long he was staying, two days before he landed. Jack offered to pick him up from the airport but he said that he had already arranged a driver. Jack tried to help with accommodation but he had already booked a stay at "The Ritz": there was nothing he hadn't taken care of already.

Isobelle was getting excited but Jack either didn't or couldn't tell her that his father was not feeling the same.

That night as he lay in bed, his thoughts turned to Autum. *It won't be long before I see her again... She knew how to charm my father and even if she doesn't want to see me, she would never let him down.*

When Frank and I arrived home, I went straight upstairs, avoiding Rosetta's welcome. I automatically went to my wardrobe to get a change of clothes before my shower, only to remember that most of my clothes had been left at the lodge. All I seemed to be doing was just looking into an empty space. Then I felt a warm hand around my waist.

"Don't worry, your clothes will be here in the morning," he said and with that, he gave me a little squeeze and kissed my cheek.

I smiled as I turned round and headed for the shower.

As I lay on the bed in my nice thick robe, Frank entered with a tray of food.

"Before you say anything, Rosetta told me to."

I laughed at how predictable I must be – she sure knows how to cheer me up when I feel low.

"I will thank her later," I said and took the tray from Frank. As I tucked in, Frank took a quick shower and joined me on the bed.

"Anything left for me?" He had a smile on his face.

"I'm not that greedy, you know! She's made more than enough for both of us." Frank ate as well and afterwards, we spent the next few hours in our room. It was wonderful but, as always, his phone started to ring and it was business as usual. I found my phone still left on the dresser. I expected the battery to be dead but Frank must have kept it charged. There were seven text messages and the answering machine message symbol was showing. As Frank paced the room talking, I lay back on the bed and went through my texts. Nothing much to worry about, a few from the girls wanting a night out, some contacts thanking me for the ball and a missed message from Frank. I then listened to my voicemails. I had two, one from my parents wanting us to come down to visit for the weekend and one from Mr Cartwright. I was taken aback by the sound of his stern voice telling me he would be in town and would like to see me. He asked me to attend lunch at The Ritz and said that a car would pick me up at 12 noon prompt on Thursday. The meeting would just be the two of us and he hoped that I would not let him down. Then the message cut off.

I looked at Frank. He was still pacing up and down talking on the phone. He turned to see me staring at him and smiled as he continued to talk.

Why is Jack's father in town? Has something happened to bring him here? Why does he want to have lunch with me? Now it was my turn to pace up and down, tapping the phone with my finger. *He knows...* A shudder went through me.

"Everything ok?" said Frank, covering his mouthpiece.

"Not really, I've had a message from Mr Cartwright."

"Should I know him?" was his response, slightly puzzled.

"It's Jack's father, he's in town and wants me to meet him at The Ritz on Thursday."

"James, can I call you back? Something's come up. Thanks." Frank crossed the room towards me.

"I don't know why he wants to meet up, unless Jack has only just told him we've split up. But that was months ago, there's no way he would have just been told."

"We're talking about Jack here, remember? He probably didn't have the balls to be upfront with this father."

"I don't know what to do." I looked for guidance from Frank.

"I'm coming with you."

"But he said..."

"I don't give a fuck what he said, I'm coming with you or you don't go." Frank was angry and it came out in his voice.

I let him calm down as I slipped under the sheets. First day back and yet more drama.

"I didn't mean to shout," said Frank. I could feel his breath against my ear.

"I know," I said and left it at that. I closed my eyes and hoped the world would just swallow me up.

CHAPTER ELEVEN

It's Thursday. Last night, I kept turning in my sleep, thinking about how today would go and wondering whether Jack would turn up.

We had breakfast in silence and before we knew it, we had headed to work and were waiting outside until the car arrived. The chauffer got out and opened the door and Frank and I stepped in, Frank holding my hand all the way, his sign of reassurance. It took just under an hour to reach The Ritz and as the car door opened, my legs went to jelly. My breathing was getting faster and it took Frank a few attempts before he finally got me out of the car.

Frank gave our names at the restaurant and we were ushered in, even though my name was the only one on the list. I keep pace with the waiter as he directs us to our table and there, waiting in his pinstripe suit, is Mr Jason Cartwright.

"Autum," he says, standing with open arms, a smile lighting up his whole face.

"Mr Cartwright, how lovely it is to finally meet you in person." We exchange kisses and I turn to introduce Frank.

"This is my husband, Frank." I watch his reaction.

He holds out his hand and gives him a quick look over before he finally says,

"Husband? I didn't know," and shakes his hand. "You're a lucky man, Frank."

Frank looks over at me and says, "I know."

"Please, take a seat. We have so much to catch up on."

As I take in Mr Cartwright's features, I see where Jack gets it from. Jason is immaculately dressed, Armani suit, expensive aftershave, designer shoes and a silk handkerchief. His hair's a mousey colour and at fifty-two he still has the charm for the ladies but a hardness when it comes to business. His eyes are a sea blue and his skin, richly tanned. His slim build suits his 6'2" frame.

"So when did you two get married?"

I look over at Frank but he answers for me.

"Nearly three months ago."

"So how long ago did you and Jack split up?" He really is in the dark.

"Sorry, Jason, but I really think you should be asking your son," I say as politely as I can.

"Don't worry. I will." His answer is sharp and to the point. I know he is upset but at least he behaves like a gentleman.

"Let's eat," he says and motions the waiter to take our orders.

We talk quite a lot and he and Frank seem to be getting on, business the main topic of conversation. After two and a half hours, we all stand up and say our goodbyes.

"It was lovely meeting you in person, Autum. I hope I get the chance to meet you again before I leave."

"How long are you staying?"

"A week, I have some business to attend to at my other office. I need to see how good my son really is. You have that advantage over me."

He means no malice in that comment, I can tell.

"I'm sure it won't be long before you see for yourself," I say and smile.

Jason gives Frank a firm shake of the hand and says,

"Make her happy, she deserves that."

"I promise I will," Frank replies and kisses me. I blush. As we head back to our driver, Jason is already on his phone, his face as stern as ever. *Must be talking to Jack...*

Jack had received a call from his father in his office telling him that he was on his way around; he thought something might have upset him but he didn't know what it could be. Jack told reception to let him know when his father had arrived so that he could greet him and show him around. He was getting butterflies in his stomach and phoned Isobelle to tell her that he was on his way to his office.

"Will you be ok?" was her response.

"Yes I'll be fine, just want him to see what a good job I've done."

"Don't worry Jack, he will. It will be fine... Love you." But Jack had already cut off the phone.

Reception had rung to say a Mr Cartwright was in reception. *The moment of truth.* Jack took in a deep breath and went down to meet him.

As Jack approached reception, his father was looking around the space and asking question to Mary at the front desk. He turned as Jack got closer and embraced him.

"Father," was all Jack could say as Jason patted him on the back.

"Son," was his father's reply.

"So what do you think? Ready for a tour before we go to my office?"

"The tour can wait. We need to talk." The sharpness of his father's tone pierced through him.

Jack felt like a little boy again, being told off for doing something. This time, he wasn't sure what he had done.

"Of course, follow me," he said and with that they both went into the lift and came out on the seventh floor. As they walked, staff gave Jack nods of the head as his father looked on. When they reached his office, his father shut the door.

"Is something wrong?"

"You tell me, son."

"I don't know what you mean." Jack was stuttering.

"Let's start with Autum..."

Jack should have expected this question but thought it would not be the first thing that his father wanted to discuss. *Did he come all the way over here to discuss her?*

"I wanted to tell you..."

"Tell me what? That she is now married to someone else?"

"How did you know that?"

"I've met him."

Jack nearly collapsed on his desk, his feet felt light under his weight. Then he started to get angry.

"What? How? I bet he couldn't wait to tell lies about me, filled your head with half truths I bet. Well in my defence, I did those things to her because I loved her and I wanted her back." When he looked back at his father, he realised that he'd dug himself a grave rather than a hole.

"What did you do to Autum?" His father grabbed hold of him and started to shake him.

"I didn't mean it, I swear."

"What did you do to her?"

"I... I kidnapped her."

"What in God's name?" He knew there was more and refused to let Jack go. "What else?"

"Please, father..." Fear laced his voice.

"Jack, son, what did you do?" was all his father could say in the most calming voice he could muster.

"I... raped her." His father let him go. Jack managed to take a breath before the shame and shock settled on his father's face.

"Rape... Autum.... how could you? Did she cheat on you? Nothing she could have done to you should have made you stoop that low!" He looked into his son's eyes and knew there was more... "Did YOU cheat on her?"

How could Jack kill his father anymore than he already had? He knew he would be doomed now. He looked down to the floor and all he could say was,

"Sorry father," his voice just a pathetic whisper.

"Are you trying to tell me that you cheated on Autum, and that she then, I have to guess, left you for Frank and to get her back, you thought you would kidnap her and then rape her? And your excuse is that you did it out of love?"

"She did try and kill me," Jack interjected, as if that would earn him some brownie points.

"I wish she had, son, I wish she had." And with that, his father left the office and did not look back.

Jack sat in his chair and for the first time in his life, started to cry. He cried, despite his tough upbringing, because he knew that his father would not forgive what he had done, no matter whom he had done it to. He cried because in his own mind, even though no one would understand, he did it because he loved her and now he had lost the two most important people in his life. But whom did he blame for this? Frank.

Jack sat there trying to compose himself. *This is your fault, Frank, you bastard. I'm coming after you and I will make sure you know the meaning of pain. If I can't have her, then I will fucking make sure she doesn't have you either. You will both suffer, I promise you that.* He threw everything that was on his desk to the floor. The office staff had started standing up to look where the commotion was coming from but he didn't care. He just got his jacket, slammed the door and headed home.

Jack checked his phone often to see if his father had called, even though he knew he hadn't. Then he kept checking that his phone was turned on, which it was. Isobelle came home all happy and excited and wanted to hear all about his father.

"So how did it go?"

"I don't want to talk about it."

"But I thought..."

"Which part of 'I don't want to talk about it' did you not understand, bitch?"

"Jack..."

"Just leave me alone." He slammed the door to the bedroom taking a bottle of vodka with him.

Isobelle was at a loss as to what could have happened. He had been looking forward to showing off the office. His father must have not been impressed with the figures and the turnover was all she could think. Little did she know...

She decided to leave Jack for a few hours but when it started to get late, instead of sleeping in the spare room, she knocked on the door and when she heard no response she went in. Jack was asleep in bed, the vodka bottle three quarters empty. *I've never seen him like this before.* She took a quick shower then returned to bed and slipped under the sheets. She felt Jack stir and turn towards her.

"Do you love me?" Jack slurred his words out.

Isobelle thought it was a strange question to ask because he knew all too well; she had told him often.

"You know I do," she said, turning to face him.

"Show me how much."

"What do you mean, 'show you how much'?" *Is this the drink talking? He isn't making much sense*, she thought.

"I want you to suck my cock."

"Jack, you're drunk." She went to turn back around and he pounced on her, pinning her to the bed.

"You're hurting me, Jack."

She could smell his vodka breath as he tried to kiss her. She resisted at first, but the more she struggled, the more friction she felt and eventually she started to like it. Bad as this may sound, she knew Jack was in a bad place. He sounded needy and she had never seen him like this. She wanted to please him in whatever way she could.

He released her hands quickly and apologised, turning to lie on his back. She immediately turned to face him leaning on her elbow and slipping the other hand under the sheets. She stopped as she felt his cock. She wanted it to be hard but it was limp. She moved her hand up and down, coaxing it to rise, as she breathed into his ear before licking his earlobe. He looked at her and sighed before he closed his eyes and started to moan, his body relaxing. She felt him harden slowly beneath her hand, then she slid under the cover to give him what he wanted. Once she placed his cock in her mouth, his legs widened and his hands were upon her head. All she could hear were the sounds he was making and him thanking her, feeding more of himself into her mouth. She knew how to suck and that's what Jack loved about her – always called her the wild one. And that's what he needed right now. She sucked his cock all the way to the back of her throat, sucked, licked and held his balls. The tip of his cock had started to spill. She used her teeth to run along his veins on its way back into her mouth and increased her speed.

Jack lifted his hips, liking the fact that she was hidden under the sheets. He was losing himself and pictured Autum sucking on him, licking him and squeezing his balls, and her face looking up at him, telling him to give her more. He raised his hips and put pressure on her head and fucked her mouth hard, thrusting in and out until he was bursting to come. When he came, he came hard and fast, his moans loud enough to fill the room, but still he kept fucking her mouth. He felt her sucking and swallowing him until he was dry, *his Autum*. Once it was over and he had stilled, he opened his eyes as Isobelle's face came into view from under the sheets. She smiled up at him and kissed him passionately before she returned to her side of the bed.

"Goodnight, Jack."

"Goodnight… Isobelle." Even then, he had to think of her name.

How could he not love this woman beside him? Isobelle had stood by him throughout everything and loved him for all his faults. She never asked for much, only hoping that one day, her and Autum would be friends again. She said it to him often, but he knew deep in his heart it would probably never happen. How could he be so cruel to her after what she had just done for him? As he turned to his side facing away from her, he mumbled "Sorry." But the real reason Jack was sorry was because he came for Autum and not for Isobelle, shame eating him up.

CHAPTER TWELVE

Frank had decided it was time he talked to his wife about having a baby. So much had happened over the past few weeks and he had wanted to discuss it with her before she had left him.

He was glad that he had had that opportunity to meet Mr Cartwright the day before. He realised how much alike he was to him: hard driven, ambitious and willing to fight for what he wanted. But then he looked at how Jack had turned out and wondered at how different two men can be. He had seen how much Jason loved Autum – his body language, the way he spoke to her, how she made him smile – and he must have been heartbroken to know that another man had taken her away from his son. *But he seemed not to have any hard feelings towards me or if he does he hid it well.*

Autum sat up, checking her emails, and Frank decided it was now or never.

"A few weeks back, after your sleepover, do you remember what you asked me?" Frank knew that was a bit of a cop out but didn't know how else to go about it.

"God, Frank, that was some time ago, we talked about lots of things."

"Yes, I know, but remember when you said the girls had been asking you about starting a family... Do you remember that?"

...I stopped what I was doing as I tried to digest what Frank was, in the worst possible way, trying to ask me. I knew this should be a serious conversation but I just wanted to laugh. He looked as if he needed me to take the lead on this so I did, but I thought adding a bit of drama to it might be fun.

"Oh, that? I'd forgotten it already, didn't think you looked interested to be honest. So don't worry, we have years ahead of us before I pop out children, lose my figure and have saggy breasts."

I looked up at Frank's face and I'm not sure if it was shock, confusion or the fact that his mouth remained open that made me want to laugh the most...

"Why are you bringing that up now?" I was trying my best not to smile.

"Oh I just thought you know, that we may, you know, start trying for you know, but it was only a thought..." He shut up.

"So what you really want to say but have messed it up big time is that you would like us to start a family?"

"Was I that bad?"

"Horrendous." We both chuckled.

"So what do you think? If you're not ready..."

"Shut up and come here," I said and planted a kiss on his lips, nearly knocking over my laptop.

"I cannot wait." And with that, we continued to kiss.

Jack eventually had a call from his father. He got butterflies at the thought of even answering it but after the fourth ring he took in a deep breath and spoke.

"Hello father." The line was quiet for a while and he realised it must be breaking his father's heart to even speak.

"Son," was all he heard back.

"I can't change what I did and I'm not proud of it. I swear to you, I have tried everything I can to get her to forgive me. I still love her and I want her back." Jack knew he was being emotional and was shocked that he had broken down to his father on the phone but he had nothing else to lose.

"Meet me at The Ritz at four." The phone line went dead.

Jack composed himself to take in the conversation he had just had. He wasn't sure of what it meant or could mean but at least his father was willing to meet him. He felt a wave of relief wash over him and quickly told Isobelle the news.

"Can I meet him?"

"Not today, we have some personal issues we need to discuss."

"Is that why you were...?" She trailed off.

"Yes, and I'm sorry for that. When my father came to my office he wasn't in the best of moods. We exchanged words and he stormed out."

"Was it because of me?"

"No, babes, it was because of... Autum."

He felt a soft hand on his shoulder and knew he didn't deserve it.

"You didn't tell him you broke up, did you?"

"No, but FRANK was more than happy to fill that part in." Jack knew he had started to raise his voice and tried to calm down.

"I don't understand. How?"

"I don't know the full story yet but I will find out at four when I meet my father. All I know is that he saw Frank before he even met his son."

Isobelle gave him a hug and they stood in an embrace for some time.

"Go into work and find out from *her* what she knew of this meeting yesterday. If she won't talk then don't worry. I shouldn't be asking you anyway, she made it clear the last time she didn't want to know you."

"She knows I'm stubborn, I don't think she will make a scene in the office." She gave Jack a kiss and got herself ready for work.

I arrive at work early, eager to tell Rebecca my good news. My face is a picture of happiness and I can't stop smiling. I settle down to work and see Rebecca enter the floor. In my excited state, I forget that she doesn't even know that I'm back. I can tell from her face that she's pleased but pissed at the same time. I stand up before she reaches my desk and block the path.

"Don't say anything just yet. Yes, I'm back. Frank picked me up and we have spent the past few days talking things through. I needed the space and I know we did not end things right on the phone, I will understand if you still think I'm to blame but I don't want to talk about that right now."

Rebecca looks at me and at first she seems unsure of what to say. But then she smiles and gives me a hug and says, "Just glad you're ok."

I hug her back, as I know we also have a lot to talk about, but for now I need to tell her my good news.

"He wants us to start a family." I nearly pounce on the poor girl.

Rebecca's face lights up and her demeanour totally changes.

"I'm so happy for you both. You deserve this. So does this mean that I'm going to be an auntie?" She starts to clap her hands.

"Shush, I don't want anyone else knowing. I just thought you should be the first to know."

Rebecca hugs me again, says, "Thanks for this," and heads towards her office. I start to work. As I watch the office slowly filling up with people, I smile, but that gets broken quite quickly when I see Isobelle walking towards me. I stand up, offish, to make her know that she is not welcome but before I open my mouth, she says,

"I hear Frank met Mr Cartwright yesterday?"

"What of it? He invited me out for lunch."

"You were there?"

"How else do you think he met Frank? Oh I get it, Jack sent you, did he? To find out what was said."

Isobelle relaxes her shoulders and lowers her voice.

"Not really, all I know is that words must have been spoken and Jack was in a bad state last night." Isobelle starts to cry and for the first time I'm out of my comfort zone and don't know how to react. I do the stupidest thing known to woman: I put my arm around her to comfort her and tell her to take a seat.

"I don't know why I'm telling you this but we did not really talk about Jack. Jason invited me out for lunch and Frank thought there might be more to it than there was. He thought Jack might have been there and he did not want me going alone so he invited himself. Once the introductions started, I told Jason that Frank was my husband." I look into Isobelle's eyes and realise how much she truly loves Jack. It must be hard for her to be caught up in the middle of this mess.

"He asked me how long we had been married and how long ago Jack and I had split up. I told him that I didn't really want to discuss it and that he needed to speak to his son and that was it, I promise." Isobelle gets up.

"Thank you" she says and walks away.

I sit back down and think to myself how much this is draining me. Every time I think nothing more will happen, it does. Why did I feel for Isobelle today? I have no idea. Granted I don't like the bitch, but even though I said I hated her, I know deep down I can't. All our lives are a mess because of one person and he seems hell bent on blaming us all to take the guilt off himself.

I continue to work and even work through lunch. There are a lot of emails to catch up on and even more apology emails to be sent. I get a call from Frank asking me if I'm working late, and even though I need to, I tell him I will meet him in the car park at five thirty. I make a few calls regarding the Birmingham office and make arrangements for me to spend some time there next week. It feels like there just aren't enough hours in the day to do it all. It's just gone five fifteen when an email pops up from Isobelle. There's nothing in the subject heading. I open it.

I just wanted to say I appreciate what you did for me today. I know it may have been more uncomfortable for you than for me, but you did it anyway.

I hate all of this, I really do, and I don't even know if you will read this, but if you do I just wanted you to know that I am truly sorry, for everything.

Isobelle

I ponder on her email for some time. Could I be a friend again after all that has happened? I email her back.

Hi Isobelle,

This is probably not the right place to be sending emails like this but I just wanted to say I too am truly sorry for all of this. You fell in love and so did I, the only difference is you were my best friend and he was my fiancé. I'm not saying it would have been different at the time but you chose not to tell me and let me find out in the worse possible way. For that, there is no forgiveness. On the other hand, I am happy that he loves you and I know just by looking at you how much you love him. I hope it works out for you both.

Can we be friends? Maybe, in time, but not just yet. I can promise you that I will be civil to you in passing on the understanding that you do not mention Jack.

Regards,
Autum

I press send and make my way down to meet Frank in the car park. When we get home Rosetta has prepared a lot more food than normal: more fish, vegetables and fruit.

"What's all this in aid of?" I ask

"We need you to be fit and healthy from now on," she says in that Spanish twang of hers.

"Fit and healthy? What for?" Then I realise.

"Has he told you?" A silly question to ask. Frank has a smile on his face as wide as the kitchen. *Does he tell her everything?* I wonder to myself.

"I've read that you need to give the baby the best start in life." He's like a kid, a very happy one.

"I'm not even pregnant yet!" I say, getting up to look for my special treats in the refrigerator.

"Where's my chocolate? And my donuts?"

"All gone. Now sit back down and tuck in."

I can see him laughing at me but I don't mind as when I do get pregnant I will demand every high calorie food going to man. *I smile* to myself.

Once we finish, I kick off my shoes and head for the sofa but Frank drags me back up before my bum hits it.

"Oh no you don't, Mrs Howard. Baby making takes a lot of practice so get up them stairs!" He gives me a slap on my bum. I let out a yelp and giggle as I run upstairs, Frank hot on my heels. By the time I hit the bedroom, Frank is already half naked and rugby tackling me to the bed. Baby making is definitely going to be fun.

Jack had received a phone call earlier on from Isobelle, telling him of the conversation that had gone on. He had not realised that his father had met up with Autum before seeing him. *Did he love her that much?* He understood then that that was why his father had been in such a foul mood on meeting him. It did serve him right, that much he would admit, for not being man enough to let his father know that they had split up. He would never have found out the reasons why if only he had been honest. But now that hole was dug, there was no getting out of it.

He felt a bit more confident meeting him again and felt he could handle whatever questions came. As he went into The Ritz and introduced himself, he was led to a quiet area just off reception where his father greeted him.

"I won't apologise for yesterday, son. What you did to that girl can never be forgiven and what she did back to you, well, let's say that was your due punishment. Frank seems like a nice man. Let's hope he makes a better go of it than you. Are you still with the woman you cheated on Autum with?" *Could he have made that sound any more vulgar?*

"Yes, I'm still with Isobelle."

"Isobelle. Haven't I heard that name before?"

"I don't think so." Jack started to get goose bumps and felt a little sweat on his brow. He tried to change the subject.

"Do you want to look around the office again before you leave?"

"Isobelle. Wasn't that one of Autum's friends?" his father said abruptly.

And there we have the final nail in the coffin. Jack paused for a moment to see how best he could reply but it was no use, he was a lamb ready to be slaughtered.

"You cheated on her for her friend? Is this what you have turned into son?"

"I have no excuse for what I have done, father, none whatsoever." Jack held his ground and spoke firmly.

His father sighed deeply and tapped Jack on his shoulder.

"I hope she was worth it."

"She was, father." And for the first time Jack actually believe what he said.

They both took some quiet time out together, then talked business on the way to the office. Jack was happy that his father was speaking to him now, happy because on showing him around the building (which was almost empty due to the lateness of the hour) that his father seemed genuinely impressed. They went back to Jack's office to talk some more and on opening the door were greeted by Isobelle.

Both Jack and his father looked surprised as Isobelle jumped up from the chair.

"Sorry, Jack, I didn't realise you were excepting company."

"Father, this is Isobelle"

"Pleased to meet you. Jack talks very highly of you," said Isobelle, walking over and shaking him by the hand.

"I'll leave you alone, I'm sure you have plenty to discuss." She moved to leave then turned and said, "It really was nice meeting you, Mr Cartwright," as she closed the door behind her.

"Big tits," was all his father said and they both burst out laughing.

When Jack got home, he called out for Isobelle. She knew something good must have happened today as she could hear it in Jack's voice.

"I think he likes you," he says, grabbing her and swinging her in the air.

"How do you know? What did he say?" she replies, giggling.

"Just said that you had big tits!" And with that, Jack laughs his head off.

"Thanks, Jack." Isobelle hits him on his shoulder.

"Believe me, he likes you," says Jack and kisses her deeply as she slides back down from his grip.

"Thank you."

"What for?"

Jack looks her straight in the eyes.

"I love you, Isobelle." He continues to kiss her but she pulls back.

"What did you just say?" She's shocked. He's never actually said that he loves her and she can't believe that this is actually happening.

"I love you too."

He lowers her gently to the sofa and says, "I'm going to show you just how much." He pulls down her panties and slides her towards him, lifting her dress up above her waist. He pleasures her with his fingers, then lowers his head and devours her with his tongue until she climaxes. He then strips off, turns her around and enters her from behind, going as deep as her insides can take him, his balls slapping against her. He pulls out when he feels that she's ready to come again and lets the feeling subside a little. He makes her straddle him, her dress and bra abandoned a long time ago. As she positions his cock near her entrance, he pulls her down onto him and enters her again, the pain shooting up her insides. She moans, his hands firmly gripping her waist, her hands embedded in his hair.

"More," she demands as she looks down at him. He thrusts harder into her and she starts to grind him; he too makes a sound. She leans into him so that he can feed on her breasts, guiding them into his mouth. He grabs hold of her bottom, pulling her cheeks apart so that she can ride him even more as he increases his pace. He feels the heat of her breath as it passes by his ear and his cock hardens for more. Her moans drives him wild as he braces himself for release. He cries out as his body starts to shake and the build up of pressure from the last few days finally gets released into Isobelle's body over and over again. She clenches tighter as she too is ready to come and lets her own juices blend with those of the man she loves.

She lay on top of him after her climax and listened to how hard his heart was beating, felt the clamminess of both skins and the precious moment they had shared, like no other time before. She had finally got her man.

Chapter Thirteen

Frank went to work with the joys of spring. He and Autum were trying for a baby and he wanted the world to know. He had promised himself that he would not ring his parents with any baby news until she was pregnant but he knew that later on that evening he would be breaking that promise. He needed to share his happiness with his parents as soon as he could and knew that Autum would understand.

When I walked into work I got straight down to business. I was preparing to go back to Birmingham and I needed to make sure there was not much left to put in place. I was still planning to come home every night but it was going to be very draining even with Rebecca at my side and a few additional staff from different departments. Some had chosen to come back at the weekends then travel back early on Monday mornings. I couldn't help but notice more people in the office expecting. *Why did I not notice them before?* I went over to Candice and asked her how her pregnancy was going. The fact that I don't usually hold long conversations probably set alarms off but I didn't even care.

"When's the baby due?" I asked.

"I leave work in three weeks," Candice said with a smile.

"Wow, you look so well. Do you know if you're having a boy or a girl?"

"A boy."

Just the way she said "boy" made me think, if I did get pregnant, how much Frank would love a son.

"Congratulations," I said and walked away. I could feel the chatter going on behind me and I knew I was the subject, but I just wondered whether I would look that good when it came to my turn. Frank was right, I wanted to be healthy – not saying I ate unhealthily – but those lovely meals at my local café would now have to be a once a month treat instead of a daily one.

It was around three thirty and I'd had no break again and enough calls from Frank to keep me busy. That's when Isobelle came walking into the office. Since I was otherwise occupied, I did not see her approach and she nearly gave me a fright.

"I won't keep you long," were the first words she spoke as I looked up.

"Is everything ok?"

"Yes, just wanted again to say thanks, I think that me and Jack, well we seemed to have turned a corner." She smiled at me.

"I'm pleased for you."

"And what about you and Frank?"

"Couldn't be better, we are trying for a baby." I know I shouldn't have said it but I was just too happy and it slipped out of my mouth.

"Congratulations, you will both make great parents and you never know, maybe I will join you soon."

"So you're trying for a baby too?"

"No, but you never know." She walked away, humming to herself.

I never thought that I could have had a conversation like that one or should I say one that did not involved food, drink or my fist flying at her face. I smile, as the different events flash through my mind. I sign off the computer, ring Frank and head to his office so that we can set off home.

I check my phone and have a missed call from Dr Hillard.

"The shrink has called me."

"Doctor." Frank shakes his head as he drives out the car park. "Is everything ok?"

"As far as I know. He must be checking to see if our appointment is still on. I will call him in the morning, it seems a bit late now.

"Nonsense, these people work nonstop. Call him now and put both our minds at ease."

The phone rings for several seconds and I'm on the verge of hanging up when I hear his voice.

"Dr Hillard, sorry to ring you so late, this is Autum Howard. Your number came up as a missed call?"

"Ah yes, Mrs Howard, just seeing if you have had any more 'dreams' since our last meeting. I know you are due to see me this week but I have to cancel as something personal has come up. Unless you can see me earlier, that is."

"I'm free tomorrow if you can fit me in at such short notice?"

"Tomorrow at six if that's not too late?" is his quick reply.

"That will be perfect. Goodbye," I say and end the call.

It feels strange, realising that I have not had any other dreams for a while. I'm happy for it to stay that way, the way I look at it, everyone is happy.

"See. Nothing to worry about." Frank slides his hand up and down my thigh, his way of reassuring me.

I start to yawn after my draining day and Frank starts to laugh as we enter our home. I can smell food waiting to be eaten as my body marches me to the kitchen. Linguine and salmon with steamed vegetables await my belly while Frank has a rump steak, boiled potatoes and vegetables. Both smell as delicious as each other. I try to take a slice of his steak but he blocks me playfully.

I go to bed happy that evening, Frank working late downstairs. Less than an hour later I have drifted off into a world full of babies, my babies.

I had given birth to twins, two boys with dark brown hair, blue eyes and olive skin, Aaron and Andrew Howard. They were a good weight when born, at four pound one ounce and three pound twelve ounces. Aaron was the bigger of the two. I remember Frank crying in the delivery room and kissing me, saying how proud he was, then the noise of two little babies and then Frank looking shocked when the nurse asked him to hold his sons. Picture perfect moment. I could feel myself laughing in my sleep.

A chill comes over me and Frank disappears from the scene and Isobelle is now there, holding my baby. I stretch out my hand and ask her to give my son back to me and she just laughs. I can't move my legs yet, still waiting for the drugs to wear off as she turns and hands my son over to Jack and they both walk out of view together, Jack's arm around Isobelle's shoulder. I scream.

That all too familiar pounding of steps as Frank burst into the room, panting like a lion that had been chasing its prey for some time.

"What is it?" he said, turning on the light.

I burst out crying as I shouted that Isobelle and Jack had taken our son. I think that even though my eyes were open I must have still been half asleep to think that I had actually given birth, never mind having twins.

"What son?"

Yep, I needed to ask myself that same question once I knew I was fully awake.

84

"Uh oh, sorry Frank, I must have been dreaming." *How embarrassing this was going to be...*

"You dreamt we had a son?"

"No, we had twins." I could picture him phoning the men in white coats to take me to somewhere safe!

"Wow," was all he could say.

It felt kind of awkward for a few moments afterwards. Frank still stood where he was by the door and I was sitting up in bed, confused.

"I'm not sure what just happened," I said, as I got out of bed and headed towards him.

"Well, from what I can gather, you have given birth to twins in the space of one hour of going to bed." A smile lit up his face.

I tried to return the smile and said, "Aaron and Andrew were their names."

"Umm, I like Aaron but we will have to work on Andrew." He gave me a hug.

"Fancy a cup of hot chocolate, with marshmallows and whipped cream?"

"What will Rosetta say when she knows that you are trying to fatten me up?"

"Well what do you think she will say when I tell her you are expecting twins!" He laughed. "Come on, let's get a nightcap. That should send you off to sleep. And if it doesn't, I know a good workout that will totally relax you afterwards."

"I'm sure you do." I gave him that raised eyebrow look as we walked down the stairs into the kitchen.

Frank talked about how he needed to spend more time with me, as promised. He said that he was going to take me back to Lincolnshire like I wanted. He then told me that he had spoken to his parents to say that we were trying for a baby and how happy they both were. I then did my own confessing about telling Rebecca and Isobelle.

"Isobelle?" He swivelled me around on my chair by the breakfast bar.

I sipped my delicious hot chocolate to delay answering him.

"Yes, Isobelle. We seem to have come to an understanding. I will be civil to her as long as she does not mention you-know-who."

"Oh, and can you trust her?"

"There will be nothing to trust her with. Once bitten, remember?" I continue to make slurping noises with my drink.

"Can I tell you something, Autum?" I look at him with concern.

"Anything, you know that."

"I too sometimes have dreams and at times my dreams seem to take on a dark side. I think they started when I first met you and you told me the things *he* did to you."

"I... I didn't know... you never said." I was so shocked with what he had told me, I didn't really know what else to say.

"You had been through a lot, still are, and I needed to be the strong one."

I want to ask him what they entailed but his mind seems to have drifted off slightly. There is a long pause before he speaks again. If I wasn't worried before, I'm worried now. *Is that why he has been working late? So that when he comes to bed he's too tired to dream?*

I smile it off as I finish my drink, finding it hard to swallow after his revelation. I'm getting sick of putting him through hell, for me. I should be over the moon, shouting from the rooftops about how happy this man has made me feel but now, on top of my dreams, I have given Frank his own nightmares to deal with.

I slam down my cup – in my head I have just put it down. The handle breaks, cutting my hand. I don't feel a thing as I get up to go to bed.

"You're bleeding."

"What? Where?"

"I knew I should not have told you anything, especially after what has happened. I'm such an idiot," says Frank as he washes the blood off.

"See. It was only a graze. Let's go to bed." My mind still doesn't register all that he's said.

Once Frank knew Autum was truly asleep, he lay on his back and thought about his own dreams. He too had seen Jack play an all too active part in them and he was always violent. Frank was starting to get the same feeling as Autum, a strange sense that something bad was going to happen. He wanted to make sure that his wife would never feel scared again. He thought about what would happen once she was pregnant. Would Jack finally let her be happy? Frank knew he wouldn't but would he do anything to hurt her and her unborn child? That was the big question and he didn't have an answer for it. He looked over at Autum sleeping and kissed her by the ear. She could feel his heat when his arm was around her, feel herself shuffling into him, moulding their bodies together as she continued to sleep.

I woke up fully refreshed from my hot chocolate nightcap and looking forward to work and to meeting Dr Hillard. I rang Rebecca to ask the girls if they wanted to go to a movie, *any excuse to pig out,* and was happy that they all agreed. We were going to a late show after I had been to see the shrink. Frank phoned me around ten in the morning saying that he needed to fly out to Barcelona for a business meeting and would be back in two days. He sounded hesitant, as if he would cancel if he thought I would worry about being alone.

"Go, Frank. You know I will be ok and if you are still worried, I will stay over at Rebecca's until you come back."

"That would make me feel more comfortable."

"That's settled then, when do you have to leave?"

"Tonight."

I was a little shocked at the short notice of it all but it must have been important for Frank to have not tried to re-schedule it.

"Sorry, but I do need to go."

"Then go, I can take the car and go to see Dr Hillard and then I will speak to Rebecca to see if I can stay at hers. It will give us some girlie time together."

"Thank you, I will see you before I go."

"You better." And with that, I could tell he felt more relaxed than at the beginning.

I went to visit Rebecca to ask if it was ok to stay over for a few days and she was more than happy for the company. She even thought it would be ideal to invite the girls to hers as well. *Let's hope we don't play anymore games.* I smiled to myself. As I was leaving, I could hear her on the phone talking to Dionne. *Wow, that girl doesn't waste much time.*

I leave the office early as I want to spend some time with Frank before he goes. He is already in a flap with his overnight bag so I take over and tell him to calm down.

"You're not usually this nervous, Frank. Is everything ok?"

He kisses me quickly on the lips and smiles that sexy smile at me.

"I just feel the timing is wrong – I shouldn't be leaving you."

"There will never be a right time with your business. If you have to go, you have to go. At least you know I will be safe now Rebecca's invited the gang round. Phone me when you arrive if you can." Soon, his packing is done, his laptop and paperwork are packed and he is ready to leave.

"I have one last thing I need to do before I leave."

Before I can ask him what it is, he is behind me, hot breath on my ear sending tingles down my spine.

"Don't you have a plane to catch?" I whisper trying not to moan as his hands move around my waist.

"The quicker you take your clothes off, the quicker I can leave." He says, starting to unbutton my blouse.

I start to get hot as the warmth spreads down me and between my thighs.

"I hope your meeting goes well." My voice starts to break and my blouse lands on the floor.

"It will once I've fucked you enough to last the two days I'm gone." I feel the zip of my skirt being pulled down and I step out of it.

He kisses my shoulders as he unclips my red lace bra and slips the straps off.

"Are you sure you wouldn't be better off with a hot chocolate?" he says as his fingers slide into my matching thong. I can feel the wetness inside.

"Always wet for me, wifey," he says, slipping his finger inside. I lean my head back to rest on him and open my legs.

"Take them off," he says, removing his finger for me to slip out of them. I hear him behind me taking off his trousers then I see his boxers flying past the corner of my eye as I remain in front of him.

"Lean back." I do and he cups my breast and slips his finger back in as I rise up on my toes and bend my knees. I try to rub against his cock as I feel it rise behind me, his breathing turning my sex up a notch more, my pussy crying out for contact by sending me throbbing messages. I turn round, his hold on me releasing, and stare into his sexy eyes. That is all it takes. My heart starts to pound as I back him straight into the wall, my tongue embedded in his mouth and Frank trying for dear life not to lose his balance. We both bounce off the wall with a jolt. I feel his teeth pinch my lip and I can taste blood.

"Are you ok?" I don't waste any time answering him, as he has two places to be: the first one is inside me and the second one is on that plane.

Frank spins me around as he grabs my butt and hoists me up as he places his cock right by my entrance. He teases it, then rubs up and down my clit, pauses a second, and before I can protest, he rams it in. I feel a sudden jolt of pain before the pleasure has time to kick in. He starts thrusting in and out, half holding me up and half holding onto the wall for support. Me, I just put my arms around his neck and squeeze my legs around him as tight as I can. His shirt's getting in the way, so when he puts me down and before he can undo his buttons I rip them apart and they fly everywhere.

"Plane, remember?" is all I say as we both pull him out of his shirt.

He carries me back to the bed as I try to get my breathing back under control.

"I want us both to taste each other at the same time, Frank." I feel a bit embarrassed asking him that as I've never wanted to try anything like that before but I do and I want it now.

"Are you sure?" I notice that his cock has no hesitation on that part as it starts bouncing up in agreement.

I lie on the bed and spread my legs and Frank positions himself over me. He lowers himself slowly but his seed has already started to spill. I'm getting so excited at the thought of my mouth around his cock and his tongue deep inside my pussy that I grab hold of it and lift my head to take it in. The noise he makes straight afterwards is priceless. Once he composes himself, his head is soon buried in my wet pussy, licking and sucking then flicking my clit, then going deep inside me. I try to moan with the pleasure of it but it's hard to do with his cock deep in the back of my throat! I raise my hips as best as I can, wanting it all, our moans blending into one as we both send each other over the edge. His cock swells in my mouth, the veins bulging from its skin and him pumping into the back of my throat. His muffled noises from below tell me he is due to come and I want to come at the same time. I open my legs even further which does the trick and as he comes spilling in my mouth, I suck him hard and fast to match his thrust and come myself, shaking, moaning and shuddering as he continues to suck me dry.

Once we had both settled enough to move, he slowly came off me, turned around and put his tongue inside my mouth, so deep and hard, both our tastes blending into one. It was so filled with love and passion and the only reason I stopped was I needed to breathe.

"Your plane?" I said

"Fuck the plane, I haven't finished with you yet." I couldn't believe it, his cock was coming back for another round, slowly swelling and rising and wanting to play some more. As for me, my pussy was saying "I so want more but I'm swollen and throbbing and need a break."

Frank climbed off the bed and pulled me down with him, my legs thrown over his shoulder, and straight away I was up for it again. *No shame.* My sex was at its full peak and he was just warming up. He leant forward, resting his arms on the bed as my legs bent with him and bang, it was in again. It caught my breath a bit as I sucked him in. Frank was going for gold and showed no mercy, his balls banging anything in sight. He was fucking me so fast that my breasts bounced up and down, nearly slapping me in the face. Sweat laced his gorgeous skin and the odd drops landed on my body. The bed was taking a battering today but no one was complaining. I started tingling inside and knew that he was hitting all the right places as my body prepared for another onslaught. I was weak with the pleasure, it was draining me to helplessness, drugging me, this from the man I love. I arched my back as I felt my climax taking over and cried out, the sucking motion of my pussy taking over as my juices started flowing again, teasing, urging Frank to follow. His noises too were getting louder and with another few fast thrusts he yelled out and I felt the warmness of his seed filling my insides. He continued to rock into me as he looked down at me, in and out, slower and slower until he collapsed on top of me.

I was too weak to move when Frank finally got up, humming to himself, and headed for a quick shower to freshen up. I managed to roll off the bed and pull out another shirt for him to wear and a fresh pair of boxers. Where he gets all that energy from, God only knows but he came out as if he had just recharged his batteries, full of the joys of spring.

"How do you do it?" I ask him.

"Do what?" he says, getting dressed.

"Nothing," I say and shake my head.

I put on a gown as I help carry his bag down the stairs, conscious that my sex is seeping, as I try to squeeze it in.

"If you need me for anything, and I mean anything, call me, ok?"

"I promise." And with those final words, we share one last kiss and the front door closes behind him.

Frank has not even driven out of the driveway when the man with the zoom lens begins to snap away, grinning. He takes out his phone and makes a call.

"He's packed a weekend bag, sir."

"Good. And the wife?"

"She's still in the house."

"Good one. Keep me updated on her whereabouts and don't let me down."

"I won't, sir." He hangs up.

CHAPTER FOURTEEN

After Frank had left, I took stock of the state of the bedroom – clothes, buttons, and underwear strewn all over the place – and smiled, the room still smelling of sex. Frank was right, I was more than full enough to last me the next two days. I headed for the shower before my visit to the shrink.

I packed a few clothes for my stay over at Rebecca's and some drink as well. I put my hair into a ponytail, threw on some casual jeans, a T-shirt and my trainers and set off. I arrived a little late and ran into the reception, apologising. Dr Hillard was already waiting there which made my embrassement even worse.

"Sorry," I said.

"You're here now. Let's get started." He waved for me to lead the way into his office, which I did.

"So how have you been since our last meeting?"

"Very well. I had no other dreams really until the day you..." I trailed off.

"The day I?" was his reply.

"Well, the day you called to book this appointment."

"Oh, so what happened then?"

I went through the whole episode from my lunch with Jack's dad to me having twins to one being taken. When I'd finally stopped blabbering, I looked up to see him writing frantically in his notepad.

"Umm, how odd," he said.

"What do you mean?"

"You seem to start off dreaming of good things, things that you want or hope will happen to you and when you are at your happiest, then your dreams turn dark, angry and upsetting. Could you be thinking these things because you feel that they may happen? Trying to predict the outcome?"

That was a new way of looking at it but why would I want that kind of outcome? I didn't even want Jack in my life let alone hurting me in whatever shape or form. I didn't really know how to respond to his question, so I pondered on it some more.

"Autum, what are you thinking?"

"Oh, sorry, I was just wondering why I would have that type of prediction. No one would want that to happen, would they?"

"No, you're right. But as far as I can see, these dreams are triggered by an event, an incident, a conversation – am I correct?"

And he was. As my mind wandered again, I thought back to how this had started, the shock of finding Jack and Isobelle together in my bedroom, the flirting at my sleepovers, the phone calls at work, the intimidation... the list went on. And what did my body do? It stored it all up for when I went to sleep.

"So how do I stop it? These people will always be around me in one way or another. I cannot avoid them or at least, not one of them anyway."

"That was not the answer I was looking for. Our subconscious mind will always find a way to plant doubt. The more you feed off it the stronger it becomes until it takes over. Why? Because you let it. Train your mind to block out the images it may put in front of you. Don't let your fear feed off you. Fight it and over time, it will disappear."

"You make it sound so easy."

"It isn't. I assure you of that. But you have a loving relationship with your husband, a family you talk about starting and a new business opening up. You're going to be a very busy woman, Autum, so use your energy to concentrate on those events, nothing else."

"I'll try, and thank you". As I got up and collected my bag, he put his hand on my arm and said, "Only you can fight this." He was right and fighting was something I was prepared to do, no matter the cost. I left Dr Hillard's office with a plan for my future and felt more reassured that things would change for the better, as long as I kept positive. I switched my phone back on once I got to the car and had a missed call from Frank. I checked the time and he should have just landed so I called him. It went straight to voicemail and I left a message:

"Hi husband, just wanted to say that I have just left the shrink's office." *I chuckled, imagining him shaking his head and correcting me with "Doctor".* "Had a very good session, off to Rebecca's so speak to you later. Love you." I blew kisses down the phone.

I turned my radio on and when I heard Jason Derulo's song "Talk Dirty" starting to play, I turned the volume up and sang, remembering what Frank and I had been doing not so long before. I tapped the steering wheel, nodding my head and moving my shoulders to the beat of the song. What a great mood I was in. I arrived at Rebecca's and she buzzed me in, my bottles clanging as I tried to open the door to get in. When I reached her floor, she had already opened the door for me. I was greeted by screams from Dionne, Emily and Imogen who already had bottles (and in Imogen's case, a can) in hand. I shook my head in disbelief as I knew we were not going out tonight. I dropped my bags, took out my own contributions and the girls went wild.

Frank had arrived in Barcelona. While he was on the plane, he had reflected on what had happened that day. The ways in which his wife got all freaky on him made him adjust himself in his seat. If this was what it was going to be like making babies he would have done it from day one, he thought, laughing to himself. He knew he was in Barcelona for business but he also wanted to buy his wife something special and he knew exactly what that would be. He checked into his hotel, dropped off his bags and asked for directions to the best boutiques in the city. The receptionist called him a cab, gave him a map and explained the directions. He was situated in the heart of Barcelona so the shops were not that far to get to. He looked at some watches to treat himself but could not make up his mind which one to choose: Bulgari, Zenith or even a Harry Wilson. He decided to clear his head and come back later. He passed some lingerie shops and of course went inside. He had thought that he would be the only man there and was quite happy that the shops were full of men and a few couples together. He knew what Autum liked, or rather, what he liked on her so headed for the cutest, skimpiest and easiest to rip off outfits that he could find. He bought three outfits in black, red and white, all lace with matching suspenders and thongs, and two Basque sets, one in red and one in black with matching briefs. Pleased with his choices, he paid and left the shop a very satisfied man. He also bought some of Autum's favourite perfume, Chanel No 5, and headed back to get a watch. He chose a Bulgari Diagono Chronograph in white gold, a bit of a mouthful but a beautiful piece of craftsmanship and well worth the price tag. On the way back to the hotel, he spotted a little shop he had not seen, hidden between the big shop frontages that dominated the high street. He went inside and the assistant greeted him with a smile.

"Are you looking for anything special?" she asked.

"No, I just wanted to take a quick look around, if that's ok."

"If you need any help, let me know," she said and walked back to the counter.

As Frank strolled around the shop, his heart started to ache. Was this what it was going to be like? He hoped so. He spent more than twenty minutes in the little shop, then went over to the counter with his purchase.

The assistant gave him another smile as she wrapped up his things in tissue paper and put them into a bag. Frank said his goodbyes and left the shop, a very emotional man.

Once back at the hotel he saw that he had a voicemail from Autum. He listened to her sexy voice and was glad that she had had a good session with Dr Hillard. He checked the time she had called and, with the time difference, knew she should still be with Rebecca so called her back.

"Frank?" All he could hear was giggling.

"I can hear you're all having fun!"

Autum giggled at the sound of his voice.

"Yes. I've arrived and as you can hear, the girls are here as well."

"Hi Frank!" was all he heard in the background.

"Say hi to the girls for me. I went out shopping today and bought you a few items."

"You mean underwear?"

"You know me so well!" He laughed, "But I have bought you some other things as well. I won't spoil the surprise until I get back home."

"Aw, thank you, I cannot wait."

"Nor can I, especially for you to try on the underwear."

"Aren't you supposed to be working?"

"Tomorrow, so tonight will give me some time to relax and prepare. Just needed to hear your voice."

Autum paused a moment.

"I love you," she said.

"I love you too. Go easy on the drink since I'm not there to seduce you afterwards."

"Will do, and keep your eyes off those Spanish girls, otherwise I may have to take the next flight out and kick ass."

"You can kick my ass anytime!" He laughed, blew her a kiss and told her how much he loved her once more.

Frank arrives for his meeting, which has been arranged by an old friend at short notice. He is ushered into the board room and waits for his friend to show up. The PA brings in a trolley which has an array of pastries and hot and cold drinks... *So this isn't just a meeting for two people, I see...*

Within minutes, his old friend appears at the door and greets Frank with open arms. He has a 5'7 frame, tanned skin and is wearing his usual 3 piece Duchamp suit. *Looking more of the playboy than I remember.*

"Hello Julian," says Frank and accepts his hug.

"Hello old friend. It's been too long." They clap each other on the shoulders.

As they part, Frank points to the trolley.

"Are we expecting guests?"

Julian looks away quickly, pours himself a coffee and takes a seat by Frank.

"Frank, there is someone who wanted to meet you. How he knew you were coming here I don't know but..." and before he can finish his sentence, the door opens and Jason walks in.

Frank abruptly stands and looks at Julian.

"I couldn't say no," he says, before Frank can ask anything.

Frank looks back at Jason, who is now taking his seat at the board table.

"Frank."

"Jason. What business brings you to Barcelona?" Frank's voice is pitched with warning.

"You are what brings me to Barcelona, Frank. You."

Julian bows out of the room leaving Frank and Jason alone.

"You don't mind if I help myself to a coffee do you. Long journey. You know how it is."

Frank does not answer but sits back down.

"I'm busy. What can I do for you?"

"Can't I relax with my coffee first? We have plenty of time for talk."

"About what?" Frank's in no mood for small talk and knows that this is no chance meeting. *Does Jason want me away from my wife? What's going on back home?*

96

"I need to make a phone call. Excuse me," says Frank and tries to move away.

"She's fine. Your wife, I mean. No need to check on her."

"I see where Jack gets his sick sense of humour from."

"That's not fair. I just want us to talk, man to man."

"And you had to get me out of the country to do that?"

He continues to drink his coffee.

"Phone her if it makes you happy, like I said I just want to talk."

Frank leaves the room and rings the security firm, telling them to watch over the girls until further notice, putting them on high alert. He then rings Autum, panic setting in when she does not answer straight away. He hangs up and rings again and this time she answers.

"Listen," is the first word out of his mouth, "Jason is here and I'm still trying to figure out what he wants but in the meantime, I have asked for you and the girls to have round the clock protection. Whatever happens, stay with the girls, do you hear me?"

I don't even have a chance to answer. As I go to move my mouth, the phone goes dead. Frank's voice was shaky. What the hell does Jason want with him? I'm not letting Frank deal with Jason alone. I know him but don't know what he's capable of. To me he seems even more powerful and demanding than Jack, which means he's more dangerous. *Fuck this.* I get myself dressed and give Rebecca the heads up.

"Where are you going?" Rebecca shouts.

"Barcelona." I slam the door behind me.

Frank heads back into the room to a relaxed Jason.

"See? No harm done."

"Let's make sure it stays that way. So what do you want?"

Jason gets up and pours himself another drink.

"Coffee. It's such a drug, don't you think?" Frank doesn't reply.

"Listen, Frank, I have been doing some checks of my own on you. You know how it goes." Jason looks up to see if Frank reacts – he doesn't. "You come from a very humble upbringing. Born in Oxfordshire, moved to London at the age of eleven, studied well and ended up at Eton, the only son of hard working parents.

"Leave my parents out of this." Frank feels his hands fisting under the table but holds on for control.

"What I am trying to get at is this: your parents did everything for you to give you what you have now. Without them pushing you and making you work hard, none of what you have now would have been possible."

"You still have not told me what you want." Frank wants to make sure that he gives as little as possible away to this man. He knows Jason has even more means than he does to get anything he wants. *And I mean anything.*

Both men have been talking for more than an hour, each one sizing up the other, but they are still no further forward than when Jason arrived in the office.

Frank gets up to leave.

"I came here to do business with Julian and not with you. If you have nothing else to say then I will be leaving."

"Sit down, I have not told you why I am really here."

"Get on with it then, I'm busy." Frank can feel the frustration in his own voice.

"Frank, are you always this rude? How do you conduct your business with an attitude like that?" He presses the intercom and asks for more coffee, fresh pastries, juice and fruit.

"I want you to leave her," he says, looking up to gauge Frank's response.

Frank laughs. "Jack getting daddy to do his dirty work for him! Such a shame it was all for nothing. You have had a wasted journey, Jason. If you think I would EVER leave my wife..."

"I'm sure I could make it worth your while."

"I don't want anything from you," Frank laughs as he stands, "After I met you, my first thoughts were how different you are to your son, YOU, the son of David and Mary Cartwright, your father a science professor and your mother... Yes, let's talk about her, shall we?" This time it's Jason who gets to his feet.

"Stop!"

"Touched a nerve did I? You see, I too did some research on Jack's famous father. Makes for a good movie, don't you think?"

"You have some nerve trying to take me on, Frank."

"And you have some nerve thinking you could bribe me to leave my wife. What I don't understand is why you think my wife would have anything more to do with your son after all the things he did to her. Or has he not told you THAT bit?"

Jason does not reply. It's almost enough to make Frank laugh. He walks out of the door and doesn't look back.

It's a long time before Frank calms himself down, pacing up and down the streets, not even looking where he's going. When he comes to, he's miles from the office and the hotel. *Brilliant... Not just Jack. Now I've got to deal with his bloody obsessed father...* The thought of Jason's offer makes Frank's blood boil again, as he starts the long walk back. The sun's begun to set when he reaches the hotel, wearily pushing open the door and tramping up the stairs. He only notices the figure by his door when he's almost touching him... *How did he find me?* Jason looks tired, maybe even apologetic. *Don't kid yourself...* Frank says nothing but unlocks his door and gestures for Jason to enter. They sit opposite each other in silence for a long time. The noises from the city leak in through the window. Finally Jason speaks.

"I know he raped her, and that sickens me."

"Let's keep to the facts, shall we? He raped her twice."

"But she did try to kill him so I think we can call it even, don't you? I want my son to be happy. That whore he's with will never be good enough for him. Autum made him happy, he is my only son and I want a grandson to take over the business."

"Listen to yourself. You're more deranged than he is if you think she would have him back. Even if she wasn't with me, she would rather slit her own throat than go back to a rapist."

The words burn Jason deeply.

"I love my son and I don't condone what he did to Autum. It makes me sick to the core to here him confess what he did to her but he will change once she takes him back. I know he will. She makes him happy, that much I know, and she would make a great mother."

"I think we are done here," says Frank. Jason doesn't move.

There was a commotion outside the doors and Frank could hear shouting and screaming. The doors burst open.

"Autum!" he and Jason said in unison.

Both men stood up shocked.

Frank waved his hand to the worried concierge to leave. The concierge looked directly at him, wanting to protest, then grabbed the door handle and shut it behind her.

Frank watched how Jason's body language changed in Autum's presence and wondered who was really in love with her: Jason or his son or both?

"How the hell did you get here," said Frank as Autum kissed him on the cheek.

"We will talk later."

"Autum, lovely seeing you again," said Jason, giving her the most melting smile known to man.

"Cut the bullshit, Jason. What the fuck is going on here?"

"We were just talking business, nothing more. Isn't that right, Frank?"

Frank was pissed as hell that she had left the country to begin with. His heart had started to race and he felt happy, angry and proud that she was here, safe with him. At least he could keep an eye on her.

"He wanted me to leave you," Frank explained sharply, "He thinks that if I leave you, you and Jack will live happily ever after and give him a grandson."

Autum was too worked up to digest fully what Frank had just said. She looked towards Jason.

"Jason, I know how much you love your son and how much he looks up to you but Jack made his choice when he went with my best friend and he made his choice when he attacked me. More than once. I could never love a man like him ever again and I would never be with a man who is capable of doing those things to me or any other woman. You need to understand we will never be together again. Never! I love Frank and plan to spend the rest of my life with him. You both need to move on and get on with your lives. He is happy with Isobelle now. She will give him children, be happy with that."

"Never. She is a glorified whore, nothing more."

I couldn't agree more, thought Autum but kept quiet.

"You need to speak to your son, Jason, he has moved on."

"Really? Well he told me that he still loves you and that he wants you back. He said he was sorry for everything he had put you through but wants the chance to make it up to you. He blames Frank for brainwashing you."

"The only thing Frank has ever done is love me like a husband, friend and lover should. I don't love your son, Jason, and I never will. Come on, Frank, this meeting is over."

"Autum, please, think about what you're saying." Jason's voice turned into more of a plea.

"Goodbye Jason." She held the door open and stared at him. After a second, Jason stood up and left the room.

Chapter Fifteen

We sat in silence, Frank holding my hand and nothing more. I didn't comment on how lovely the hotel was, or the city, I just sat, Frank's heavy breathing the only thing keeping me company. Slowly, he came out of the daze he had found himself in. He opened his mouth to speak but then just stared at me.

"Frank," was all I could say. I knew he might be mad at what I'd done but I needed to tell him why I'd done it.

"How did you know where I was?"

"Your diary and flight details were left in the study. Listen, Frank..."

"No, please let me speak. I was so mad when I saw you burst through those doors. I thought damn woman, doesn't she know when to listen? But then I was glad in a way. Jason was not listening to anything I was saying – I walked away from him at the office but he wouldn't quit. He was waiting for me here. But by you being here and Jason hearing those things from your mouth, maybe he'll realise the truth."

"You scared me when you phoned. I couldn't stay there not knowing what was going on. I'm sorry I didn't tell you I was coming, Frank, but you never gave me the chance." He gave me a hug.

"God, will you ever stop amazing me, woman?"

"Never." As he hugged me, I peeked over his shoulder and saw the bags on the bed. I pulled away and headed for them.

"Hey, no peaking! I said 'when I get back home', remember? Talking of home, when are you flying back?"

"The same time as my husband of course. Thanks to his credit card." I laughed.

"Well you need to pay me back every penny, woman, and I know just how you can make your first payment."

With that, he let me make my way over to the bed to look into the bags. I took out a thong with my finger and gave him that look. He smiled.

"Payment number one is due today or else the outfits go on and interest will start to accrue."

"You know I don't have any money on me," I said as he took off his jacket, slightly loosened his tie and unbuttoned the top of his shirt. He sat down on the chair, like he was waiting for some private show.

"You better start getting undressed then. I'm a busy man, you know? People to see, wife to fuck... it's a hard life but someone has to do it." He laughed.

"Frank, when did that mouth get so dirty?"

"Interest rates are hitting an all time high..." He tapped his watch.

I took out some of the outfits. How can I describe them? Oh I know... Umm, how can I put this? Oh yes: less was definitely more where Frank was concerned!

As I ploughed through the other bags, Frank darted up.

"Not that one!"

But by the time he'd reached the bed, I had already pulled the gift out of the bag and started to take it out of the tissue.

"Oh God, Frank, you, you bought..." I sat down on the bed and started to cry. They were just so beautiful.

He came and sat beside me, hand around my waist, as we looked at the two garments on my lap, beautifully made, soft to the touch and each embroidered with a beautiful name.

"Aaron and Annabelle." I looked up at him

"I couldn't resist them. After all, you did say twins."

I gave a little chuckle remembering my dream.

"I know it may be too soon."

"I love it." I continued to stare at my first baby outfits, wiping the tears from my eyes.

"When the time is right, there will be tears of joy for both of us." He wiped a tear building up at the corner of his own eye. "Now let's lighten the mood, starting with those outfits."

Jason sat in his boardroom thinking about Autum's words to him. He'd been shocked to hear the tone in her voice when she spoke but was he angry? Far from it. But it made how he felt about her that bit more challenging. He wanted to own her, that he knew, but using Jack's feelings for her had backfired.

She's mine, he thought to himself and felt ashamed of why he was drawn to her that much. He knew it wasn't sexual yet he still couldn't describe it. Even though they had talked often via video link in Jack's office, he had never realised how truly amazing she was until he met her in the flesh. He was angry that Jack had thrown it all away for that trash he now called a girlfriend. He knew he stood no chance playing fair, but the way he looked at things, money could buy you anything and anyone if the price was right. He smiled to himself and took out his phone to make some calls. He needed to get back on his private plane and head back to London. His work was far from done; it was only just beginning. Frank was a good match for her and he liked him for that. He never admired weak people and Frank would not be easy to break. Why were his feelings so strong for her? He didn't know but he wanted to apologise for how he had behaved just so he could see her again and smell her beautiful perfume. *Chanel No 5*: it was so unmistakeably elegant, just like her. He knew how he was going to see her again. All he had left to do was put his plan into place and choose the place and the time. Then he would finally get want he wanted and be in her company again.

Jack got a call from his father saying that he was flying back from a business trip and that he wanted to meet him at his office. He made it clear that he did not want any disturbances and that Jack should get his secretary to cancel any bookings for the rest of the day.

"Can I ask what the urgency is?"

"All in good time, son," was all Jason was willing to say.

Jack was very curious. It was very rare for his father to sound so mysterious over the phone as he was a straight talking kind of guy. He had already confessed to his father about what he did to Autum. Perhaps his father wanted to discuss his relationship with Isobelle. That made Jack smile: he now felt like he could actually move on. He knew that his feelings for Autum would never change but he wanted to let his feelings for Isobelle develop. She deserved that at least.

At lunchtime he met up with Isobelle at the local sandwich shop and ordered a sweet chilli chicken wrap with a fajita dressing and salad, while Isobelle ordered a chicken and mango sandwich with jalapenos.

"I may be home late today. My father has called an emergency meeting at the office. Unsure what and how long it will be for."

"Is everything ok?"

"As far as I know." He took a bite of his wrap, licking the sides of his mouth in the process. "Anything interesting happening at work?"

"Not much really. A few girls planning holidays... A wedding... oh and I forgot... Autum and Frank are trying for a baby."

Jack spat out his food, choking.

Isobelle got up and started to pat his back, his face going as red as a beetroot as he continued to cough.

"A baby?" he said, recovering, "Isn't she too young for all of that stuff?" He was trying to sound as if it didn't bother him but deep down it was killing him. Once she was pregnant, there would be nothing left for him to hold onto, nothing.

"Oh Jack, she's married now and most people once they get married tend to have babies! You so need to keep up." She continued to rub his back.

Once Jack got his breathing under control, he took a sip of his drink to clear his throat.

"How do you know all this? Office gossip, I suppose?"

"Nope, she told me herself. We are getting on better now. Still a long way to go but baby steps, you know? Do you get it? 'Baby steps'" She started to laugh as she finished her sandwich.

Jack got it all right and it nearly choked him.

Jason arrives back in London to meet his son. He makes his way up to his office and lets himself in. Jack stands to greet his father.

"You need to dump her. NOW." Jason takes a seat.

"Dump who?"

"Isobelle. She's not right for you, son, and you know it. Your heart will always love Autum and no one will come close to her. Isobelle is good looking trash, nothing more."

"Father, I won't."

"You will or I will do it for you. The choice is yours."

"What's brought this on? What have you done?"

Jason pauses for a moment.

"I met up with Frank again and I told him to leave Autum."

"What? Why would you do that?"

"I did it for you. I know how much you love her and I thought if I reasoned with him..."

"You mean you tried to bribe him?"

"Whatever. I tried to reason with him, even waited for him at his hotel, then a surprise guest burst in."

"What do you mean a surprise guest?"

"Autum."

"This just gets better. And where was all this going on?"

"In Barcelona."

"I'm not even going to ask... Listen, father..."

"No, you listen. Dump the bitch and do whatever you need to get her back. UNDERSTOOD?" And with that, he begins to walk away.

"It's too late for that. They are trying for a baby."

Jason turns to look at his son.

"Trying, son. Trying. Remember that." He walks out the door.

Jack was angry that his father had called Isobelle "trash". He also couldn't understand the desperation in his father's voice for him to get back with Autum. Why was he pushing it so much? *I'm trying to start afresh, father. Don't do this to me, not now.*

Jack had thought that his father might, in time, come around to liking Isobelle. How wrong he was. All Jack knew was that he was, for the first time, happy, yes happy, and turning his life around. He couldn't go on obsessing about someone he knew he had finally lost... *or had he?*

CHAPTER SIXTEEN

I had headed to Birmingham with Rebecca and a few staff to start the next phase of getting the office up and running. I had had such a great few days and even though I hadn't planned to, it had been well worth it.

When I returned from Barcelona, I checked on Rebecca and the girls, told them how Frank finally forgave me for crashing the party and apologised to the security firm for leaving the country. Nothing could spoil the mood that I was in. I had packed for the first week in Birmingham and was going to travel daily after that. My parents wanted to spend some time with me and Frank and the coming weekend was perfect.

Our hotel was based inside The Mailbox so everything was on site, so to speak. Rebecca and I settled in with our co-workers and welcomed the new staff heading through the doors. Once the meet and greets were out of the way, it was business as usual and staff were sent into different rooms to begin their weeks of training. I made a few phone calls to some suppliers but besides that the day went by quickly.

It was four thirty before we ended work and headed back to our room. I was so exhausted that after we'd eaten in the restaurant, I wanted to call it a night.

My phone rang around nine and I answered it quickly.

"Hi, honey."

"It's Jack. Please don't hang up, I promise I won't cause any trouble. I just want to talk."

"I thought your dad did the talking for you."

"I knew nothing about that. I hope you believe me." And for some reason I actually did.

"What do you want to talk about, Jack? I've had a long day and I'm tired."

"I know I have said this before but I am really sorry for everything that I have done to you. I cannot move on until I know that we can put our differences behind us."

"Jack, please."

"I mean it this time. I will always love you. That will never change but I also know that what we had, I will never have again."

"I'm glad you realise that. Just make sure that you treat Isobelle well. She loves you."

"I know. It took some time for me to realise that but I will look after her, I promise."

"Good. I need to go now, Jack."

"Before you go, I need to know we're ok."

"I cannot say that, Jack. Too much has happened between us that I cannot forget or forgive. When I think nothing else can happen, you throw something else in the mix." I started to get emotional.

"I'm upsetting you. I'll go."

"Jack, it's not that..." I never got a chance to finish my sentence. He hung up on me.

I took a shower and flopped on the bed exhausted. I chatted to Frank briefly before I realised I hadn't heard half of what he was saying. When he told me to have an early night, I was glad to comply. I wrapped myself around my pillows, fell asleep and started to dream.

I was out with the girls, having seen a West End show. We drank until the early hours. We'd taken in a few cocktail bars and then gone to a salsa bar. It was loud, it was full and there was plenty of dancing going on. We settled into a spot near the dance floor and Rebecca got a round of drinks in. Someone held out a hand and motioned for Rebecca to hit the floor and we all encouraged her to do so, laughing all the way. Then it was Dionne and I was left swaying by myself until I felt someone's hand around my waist. I turned to look at him. He was tall, very orange, or should I say, extremely tanned in a bad way, with a smile that could light up a room and a body to die for that I could see through his open front shirt. As I try to remove his hand, he draws me nearer until we are but a breath apart. I go to open my mouth in protest at this invasion and I feel a pinprick in my neck. It all goes dark.

I wake up quickly, panting, no Frank or Rebecca to console me. I recall most of the dream but again don't understand it. I rub my neck as if I can still feel where the needle went in. Was someone try to drug me? But he was a stranger, no one I knew and with no link to Jack. It just did not make sense.

The hotel phone took pleasure in telling me it was six thirty in the morning as I dragged my sorry ass into the bathroom. I needed to wake up but I just wasn't feeling it. I jumped into the shower and felt the first burst of hot water hit my hair and face. I gasped, the power from it was so good, I felt as if I was having a shower and massage at the same time. As I closed my eyes and just stood there for a moment I sensed that I was being watched. I can't describe the feeling but it was strong and overpowering to the point I was scared to open my damn eyes. How silly does that sound?

I covered my body as much as I could with my hands before I opened my eyes and looked around the steamy room. "Hello," I shouted as if I expected someone to reply. Well if someone had replied, then I would have truly shat myself. Stepping out of the shower slowly, I grabbed my towel and wrapped it around myself, letting my hair drip down. I left the shower running to hide the noise of me creeping out. I headed for the bedroom, my heart really going for heart attack of the year award, my pulse trying to pop out of my neck with fear. I tried not to blink or breathe as if I did I might miss something or make too much noise. I was such a mess. The bedroom was large enough, like most hotel rooms, but no one could jump out and get me from the angles of the room without me seeing them, which made me less anxious. Once I was happy that there was no one there and I had triple checked that I had locked and bolted the door, I finished off my shower and got ready for work.

I remembered what Rebecca had told me before that something was triggering these events and she was right. I had only spoken to Jack the night before and then BANG, the dream. I just felt like I was being watched by an invisible presence. *I had to control my thoughts.* If I could master that I could win.

After breakfast and a few strong coffees, we all went into work together. I settled into my office and could here the hustle and bustle of things going on around me: the office getting its final touch ups, the phone lines being tested, the air conditioning going on and off. It was all a nice distraction and that's how the week went on. It was now Thursday and Rebecca had left with the girls to go back to the hotel. I wanted to put some reports and plans together so I'd said that I would meet her for dinner at eight thirty.

The office was eerily quiet but it was nice and I was getting much more work done with no distractions. Then I heard footsteps

I started to smile, *Rebecca is so forgetful sometimes*, and didn't look up, just said,

"What have you forgotten this time?"

"Nothing," was the reply. A deep voice. A man's voice.

I looked up to find Jason with a bouquet of flowers and a Chanel shopping bag.

"Jason, what are you doing here? How did you know where I was? I…" and I trailed off, too stunned to think of any more words.

"I wanted to apologise for my behaviour in Barcelona. I should never have said those things to Frank. It was not my place."

"No, it wasn't. But I still don't understand why you are here."

He came towards me and handed me the flowers.

"For you. My way of saying sorry."

I took the flowers from him. They were so beautiful. My favourite long stem white lilies, with white roses and greenery. The bunch was so big I had to use two hands to support it.

"They're beautiful, Jason, but you shouldn't have."

I put the flowers on my desk as he handed me the bag.

"What's this?"

"This is also for you, as a way of saying that I am really, really sorry. If the flowers weren't enough for you to forgive me, I am hoping this will be." We both laughed.

Inside the bag was a large white box with a thin black line surrounding it, the label, as I had guessed, read "Chanel". There were perfumes, soaps, lipsticks, eye shadows and a purse spray.

"Jason, this is… this is too much. I cannot accept this." *God, I could so take this but I should at least pretend that I can't.*

"You don't like it." He looked totally stunned.

"I love it but…"

"Then please accept it. It will make me happy. Please."

I went over and placed a kiss on his cheek.

"Thank you," he said

"What for?"

"Forgiveness. Well I hope that meant you have forgiven me." A smile formed at the corner of his mouth, his heart warming at the same time.

"Have dinner with me."

I looked into his pleading eyes, paused for a moment then accepted. What harm could it do?

We go to an Indian restaurant a short drive away and manage to get in without a reservation. The room's décor is beautiful.

"You were quiet in the car."

"I was thinking of how you got here but then I thought about how you got to Barcelona and realised it was not worth asking."

"I'm a man of many means." He smiles

"I'm beginning to find that out." I smile back up at him.

"Ready to order?" I nod.

"I need to make a phone call; I told Rebecca that I would meet her for dinner at eight thirty."

"Tell her you've met up with a friend. If you tell her you're with me, Frank will have the armed guards after me."

I dial her number and wait for her to answer.

"Rebecca, it's me. I err…met a friend and will be having dinner with them."

"Where are you, you sound funny?"

"I'm fine, don't worry. I won't be back late. I'll check on you when I come back."

"Something's wrong. Is Jack there? Talk to me, Autum."

"I'll see you later." I hang up.

"You know she will be ringing Frank now, don't you?" says Jason and a split second later my phone rings.

"I can't lie to him, Jason."

"I don't expect you to. Let me speak to him."

"No" I say sharply, and he snatches the phone from my hand.

"Autum, what the hell is going on?" says Frank, "I've had a hysterical Rebecca on the phone saying you're with Jack."

"Frank, calm down. She is just having dinner with me."

"Jason, what the fuck are you doing there? If you hurt her, I will kill you."

"Calm down, Frank. Here she is, ask her yourself. We're in a restaurant surrounded by people trying to have some dinner." He hands me back the phone.

"Frank, calm down, I'm ok. He came to say sorry about Barcelona."

"Don't trust him, Autum. Please, get out of there now."

"Frank, you're scaring me."

"Autum, he's in love with you."

"What?"

"He's as dangerous as Jack. Believe me, please."

I look at Jason and see a look I've never seen before. His eyes appear darker than normal and his body now seems rigid. I stand to leave.

"Where are you going?" He stands as well.

"I have to leave, Jason. Sorry." I can hear Frank still on the end of the phone.

"I understand. At least let me take you back to your hotel."

"No!" Frank shouts.

"I'm good, thanks." I make a steady retreat out of the restaurant. I tell Frank that I have hailed a cab but that Jason has followed me outside. I start to panic. As Jason creeps up beside me a small yelp leaves my mouth.

"You scared me."

I put the phone close to my chest, knowing Frank is still listening.

"What did Frank say to you to make you want to leave in such a hurry?"

"It doesn't matter, Jason."

"Whatever it was startled you, at least give me a chance to defend myself."

"He said you're in love with me." I look him straight in the eye to see his reaction.

"I think you husband has an over active imagination, don't you?" He laughs.

Frank is never wrong about things, why would he say that unless he knew something I didn't? I raise the phone to my ear.

"Autum, find someone and stay with them until your cab comes. Do not leave with him, ok?"

"I promise. I love you, Frank."

"Stay on the phone, Autum. Do not cut me off until I know you're safe."

"Promise."

I move away and talk to some random strangers, asking how long it takes for cabs to come, talking about the weather and whether they have been to The Mailbox. Anything to pass the time.

"I cannot leave you until I know that you have got into a cab safely," says Jason. I feel bad that I can't trust him but I know I can't. I smile off his gesture and thank the gods when a black cab pulls up.

"Thanks Jason, I will be fine now." I step towards the cab.

"So sorry, Autum. It wasn't supposed to be like this."

I turn to ask him what he's on about and feel a quick prick at the side of my neck.

"What the hell have you done to me? Frank! He's... He's done something... and... and I can't stay awake." I feel Frank's voice fading and the phone slipping from my hand.

"You pushed me, Frank, and now you'll suffer. You're good but I'm better. Don't forget that."

"You want to punish me, then take me. She's suffered enough. Let her go."

"Don't worry, you will both suffer." Jason throws the phone on the ground and stamps on it.

"She's had one too many, you know what I mean? Fresh air's kicking in now," he tells the cab driver, "I'll take her home." With a nod, the cab drives off. Jason carries me to his car and that's the last thing I remember.

Chapter Seventeen

Frank was left stunned, his heart pounding out of control. He walked up and down in his study, his blood starting to boil as the rage overtook him. He cried out with a loud growl, knocking everything off his desk and throwing anything his grip could get hold of before he slumped to the floor. Rosetta ran into the room to find him bent over and crying.

"Get out," he shouted, waving her away and without a word she ran. He got up and phoned Rebecca.

"Why the hell did you not stay with her? That bastard has got her. She could be anywhere."

"Jack is in Birmingham?"

"His fucking father." He hung up. Frank composed himself enough to get his keys and stormed out of the house not even shutting the door behind him. He got into his car and headed for the only place he knew where he might find some answers. He parked his car outside Jack's apartment not caring how it looked, ran to the entrance and pressed the buzzer for Jack to let him in. Isobelle answered.

"Hello?"

"It's Frank, let me in."

"What's wrong?"

"Just buzz me in, I need to talk to Jack. It's urgent."

"Err, I'm not sure, Frank."

"It's important!" He heard the loud buzz and ran up the stairs. When Isobelle opened the door, Frank burst in.

"Where is he?" asked Frank as Jack came into the hallway. Before Jack could reply, Frank lunged at him and caught him right on the nose, drawing blood.

"What the fuck?" was all Jack could say before Frank took another swing at him. Blood spilled everywhere and Isobelle started to scream.

"Where has he taken her?"

"What the hell are you talking about? I think you've broken my nose, you bastard!"

"I'm the bastard?" He hit him hard in his stomach. "Where is she?"

Jack was curled up on the floor clutching his nose and holding his stomach with his other hand, Isobelle helping to stem the flow of blood. It was only then that Jack realised who Frank was talking about.

"Autum?"

"Yes. My wife. What has he done with her"

"Frank, you need to stop yelling. Who has taken her? I don't know what you're talking about."

"Your God damn father, that's who. Now where the fuck has he taken my wife?"

Jack was now bloodied and confused.

"Why would my father take her? I don't understand."

"You're both fucked up. What is there to understand? Phone him and find out where he is holding my wife."

Jack made his way back into the living room with Frank hot on his heels, making sure that no conversation was held without him hearing it.

"Make sure you put him on loud speaker," Frank said, pacing as he spoke.

As Jack dialled his father's number, Isobelle offered Frank a drink, which he declined.

"He has no involvement in this, you know? He is as shocked as you are."

Frank gave her a cautious look telling her to back off. She read him loud and clear and moved away. The next thing he heard was Jack speaking.

"Father, what have you done?"

"Ah son, I see you've spoken to Frank."

He could see Frank charging to take control of the phone and he shushed him to be quiet.

"Where is she, father? Is she alright?"

"You know I could not harm her. She is fine – sleeping as we speak."

"Where is she, father?"

"She's safe, that's all you need to know. I forgot how beautiful she looks."

"Touch her and I will kill you."

"Ah Frank, I knew you wouldn't be far away. Maybe the two of you should work together in finding your wife and your... love interest, son."

Jack felt the heat rush to his cheeks, knowing Isobelle was right at his side.

"I told you, I've moved on. Stop stirring up trouble."

"Keep kidding yourself, son. You will never inherit anything whilst you're still with that whore. Yes, I know you are there, Isobelle. I can smell your cheap perfume even through the phone." And he laughed.

"How dare you!" she hit back.

"How dare you think you can fuck my son and... what? Live happily ever after? How can someone like you, who was so quick to cheat on her best friend with her fiancé, ever be loyal? Don't make me laugh."

"Jack, don't let him speak to me like that! Say something."

Frank grabbed the phone. "I don't give a rat's arse about Jack and Isobelle's relationship, I'm here to find my wife."

"You're a clever man Frank, that's why I know you will find her. Your love is strong, stronger than that of my son. You will fight for her, something I wish my son had done – then maybe he could have got her back before you came on the scene. Work together and she will be returned safe and sound. Work apart... well, you don't need me to finish, do you? I give you my word as a business man, I will not harm her. Son, I know how passionate she made you feel. YOU may turn out to be the hero." That was Jason's last word before he hung up.

Jack thought about his father's word – "hero". *My father wants me to be his hero. I promise, father, I won't let you down.*

Isobelle was still crying on the sofa while Frank was talking to Jack.

"How can a family be so fucked up?" Frank looked Jack in the eye. "Not only did she struggle to get over what you did but now your fucked up father has decided to take over where you left off. How much does he know?"

"I told him everything but he disciplined me for it. He was even ashamed for a short time at what I did. There is no way he would hurt her."

"He won't hurt her; he's in love with her."

"Don't be so absurd." Jack stood up in defence.

"I watched how he reacted every time she was in his presence. At first I dismissed it as madness but now I know. He fooled me into going to Barcelona just to tell me that, kept telling me to leave her so that she would fall back into your arms." Frank laughed. "What we both didn't realise was that my wife had flown over – she burst into the room and put him straight."

"You didn't know she was coming?"

"Of course not. She took us both by surprise but I was glad she came so that he could hear it from her mouth that she would rather kill herself than go back to a rapist." Frank felt no love for Jack and every word he spoke was laced with hate.

"Get your coat, we're leaving." Frank stood up and waited for Jack to do the same.

"I'm coming with you. Despite what you think I still care about her and you know that," said Isobelle, looking at both men in turn.

"Do what you want, I'll meet you downstairs," said Frank, leaving.

Jack grabbed a jacket and Isobelle did the same and they chased after Frank. By the time they'd reached the front of the building, Frank was tapping on the steering wheel impatiently. Jack sat in the front and Isobelle took the back seat, her belt not even fastened when Frank took off, at speed.

"Start talking," Frank said.

"What do you want to know?"

"Where would he take her?"

"How the hell would I know? This is his first visit to Britain, remember?"

Frank pinched the bridge of his nose and sighed.

"Think, God damn it. You must know something about your father's properties."

"You need to swing by my office. I can make some phone calls. He was due to go back home soon so his office must know something."

Frank had no choice. He was totally reliant on Jack and he hated it but he would do and put up with anything to find his wife. He continued to drive at speed.

They arrived at Jack's office and security let them in. Frank looked around, impressed with what he could see. Jack told them to help themselves to coffee which they did as he pulled out his diary, turned on his laptop and started to make some calls.

"I can't begin to know what is going through your mind, Frank, but if you need to talk..."

Frank turned to look at Isobelle but did not reply.

"How long will you ignore me? We're in this together."

"Together?" He was on the verge of a hysterical laugh. "Are you really that delusional? All this started because of YOU. My wife's nightmare started with YOU and if anything happens to her, it will be because of YOU." He got up and moved away to calm himself down, Isobelle sobbing on the sofa.

In the background, Frank could here Jack on the phone.

"So you say he went to look at a large property?" He started to scribble on a piece of paper. "And where is this property based?... Uh huh.... hired it out indefinitely?, Thank you so much Grace, you have been most helpful." He ended the call, excited at the news.

"We may have our first lead." He picked up the piece of paper that he'd written on, "My father has rented a large house in a place called Romsley in the West Midlands. It should take no more than two hours to get there." He looked over at Isobelle.

"Why are you crying," he said as he put his arms around her.

Isobelle looked up at Frank as she stood.

"I'm fine. Let's just go, shall we?"

CHAPTER EIGHTEEN

I woke up with a bit of a headache, disorientated and weak at the same time. At first, everything was still hazy and it took a while for things to come into view. When they did, I lifted myself up to find that I was on the most luxurious bed, soft and warm, goose feather pillows under my head, my body wrapped in Egyptian cotton sheets, thick shag pile carpets covering the floor. My movements were slow as I slowly turned to come off the bed. My clothes had changed and I was barefoot. *The bastard undressed me.* I start to walk quickly, too quickly, and stumble but compose myself to head for the door. It's locked.

"Jason, Jason, let me out!" I bang on the door but start to feel sick and head for the bathroom just in time for my stomach to start to wretch. I throw up all over the toilet. When it finally stops, I splash cold water on my face and rinse out my mouth. Then I hear a click of the latch and look up to see Jason walking through the door.

I charge at him.

"You bastard! Where am I?" I hit him in the chest with my fists but he grabs hold of my wrists.

"Calm down. You're safe."

"Safe? How can I be safe when you trick me, lock me up and take off my clothes?" I try and struggle from his grip.

"I did not take off your clothes. What do you take me for? A girl friend did it for me."

"Liar – that's what you are. You're just like your son." I spit out the last few words.

"I'm nothing like him."

"Where am I? What do you want from me?" I start to sob, my arms flopping as he loosens his grip on me.

"I will not harm you, I promise. This is about Jack and Frank working together to find you. This is about the two men in your life that love you endlessly and will do everything in their power to find you."

I pause for a moment and digest what he has just said.

"You're playing a fucking game?"

"Call it what you like. My son has never stopped loving you. He will fight for you until the end."

"End? Fight? God, Jason what's happened to you? There will be no 'me and Jack'. I will not be part of your games." I try and walk off.

"You already are. They're on their way as we speak, Isobelle tagging along for the ride."

"Did you tell them where we are?"

"No. My secretary Grace did that for me." He laughs. "Now let's eat, I have prepared a late snack for you."

"I'm not hungry."

"I wasn't asking." He steps aside so that I can pass him, stomping and huffing like a child.

The dining area is large and very formally set for two. There are lamb shanks, salmon, steaks, vegetables, salads. I'm just not sure if this is going to be my last meal.

I eat but never take my eye off Jason. It's only when I'm half way through my meal that it hits me that my food could have been drugged. I spit out what's in my mouth.

"Didn't you like your steak?"

"I did until I realised you probably slipped something into it."

"Do you want to swap so that I can prove to you there is nothing to fear?"

"How can you say that after what you've done? And you still have not told me where we are and how long you plan on keeping me here."

Jason continues to eat and ignores my questions.

"Fine." I get up.

"Where are you going?"

"I guess you have locked me in so I am going back to my room, the room you will probably lock once I'm in there."

"Sit back down."

"No."

"SIT." His voice is deep, loud and threatening.

I go over to him to challenge him, feeling braver than I look, and slap him across the face.

"Feisty." He rubs his cheek. "I can see what Jack saw in you." I want to scream and shout at the man in front of me but I decide he may be getting some sick kick from my anguish so I turn my back on him and walk away.

"Deny it all you like, Autum, but I know you still love Jack. It will only be a matter to time before I prove it to you."

I pause for a moment with my back to him. *They're in this together, I should have known.* I continue to try and leave the room when Jason talks again.

"Talk to me."

I realised something: Jason has been away from his son for so long he doesn't know what his son is actually like.

"Why Jason, I never thought you were like him. I thought YOU of all people would keep him on the straight and narrow. He looked up to you and I thought you were proud of him. He worked so hard in making the business work, not for me but for you. Then you come over here, your first visit to England, and instead of working and getting closer to your son, you do this – waste all your time kidnapping me, thinking that I will be so glad when Jack 'rescues' me that I'll give up the one relationship that has ever made me happy with the man I want to spend the rest of my life with and have children with. For all I know, you and Jack hatched this plan together. I respected you before but now I can barely look at you."

"I'm not a bad man. Since I have been here, I've changed but I don't know why. I love my son for all his faults and even now I still protect him. I love you, Autum, as a daughter-in-law. I don't want to lose you and nor does my son. I forgave him even though it sickened me to my stomach to find out what he did to you. I even said I wished that you had killed him."

I know that it's hurting him to tell me some of this but does he need to go to these extremes? I'm shocked at his last statement and feel his pain.

"Jason, can I ask you something?"

"Go ahead."

"If you loved someone so much that you planned on marrying them and then you found them with your best friend in your house and in your bed, would you still want them back? And then, if for good measure they drugged and raped you, all in the name of love, would you still want them back then?"

"Stop, please."

"Answer me."

"Of course not. I know what you went through. I've been through it myself. That bitch I married wanted my money but not my love. Time after time, I took that bitch back, thinking she would change but she continued, until I threw her out and never looked back."

"Wait, Jack never said. I thought you just drifted apart."

"I never told him the extent of the things she did. He loved her and I did not want him to grow up hating her and blaming me. So I made her out to be the perfect mother and wife, then said that we just grew apart to soften the blow."

"But she never came back for her son."

"Why would she? She found another billionaire to bleed dry."

"Is that why you're so…"

"Cold? Say it."

"Sorry, Jason."

"Don't be. I'm not." He walks off to get a drink.

"I think I need one myself." I'm hearing revelations not even Jack knows.

"Was Jack in on your plans for me?"

"No, he knows nothing of what I was doing. I really wanted things to work out for you both. I know, I know, it would never work. I just missed our video conference calls. They were the only things that kept me going after a bad business meeting. I just missed you brightening up my day and it made me proud that my son had found someone like you. But tell anyone that I'm a softie and I will be after you!" We both laugh.

"Do you think they will be coming to get me?"

"There're already on their way, should be here soon. I don't expect Frank to understand what I did and I know that this must be as much as a nightmare for him as it is for you and I am sorry for that. When they arrive, I will leave for the airport and you will never see me again, I promise."

I rub the top of his shoulder with my hand.

"You need to sort things out properly with your son before you leave."

"I know, but what if he…"

"He won't."

"How can you be so kind to me after what I have done?"

"I just want to go home, have a hot bath and forget that this ever happened. If you ever trust someone again – and I hope you do – like me, you will find your soul mate. Don't go looking for it, Jason. It will happen when you least expect it. Don't fight it, just let it happen, ok? And remember, you don't need to go to these extremes to have a conversation." Again we both laugh. "I'm tired, Jason. I'm going to bed. And I think you could do with some sleep yourself."

"I can't. They should be here in the next thirty minutes or so. I need to let them in."

For a split second I had forgotten about Frank, Jack and Isobelle coming here.

"Isobelle loves him, you know? If she makes him happy then let them make their own mistakes. He will always be there for you. Don't force him to choose. Just say they have children – do you really want your son to stop you seeing your grandchild?"

"But she's not you."

"And she will never be. Accept that. Your son is happy."

I go and give him a hug; I think we both need it.

"I'll stay up with you."

"No, you sleep. I'll wake you when they arrive."

"I'll get a blanket and meet you back in here."

"You really are stubborn. Poor Frank."

"Frank tells me that all the time." I laugh.

CHAPTER NINETEEN

Frank had been driving for nearly an hour and a half when Isobelle asked to take a break. They stopped off at a service station and Frank got himself a strong coffee, knowing the night was only going to get worse. *Are we in this together? That's the main thing. It all seems too easy that the first phone call he makes, we happen to find out where his father's rented. Having to put my trust in him doesn't sit well.* Frank could not even remember most of the drive so far, his mind preparing him for different scenarios, his heart beating a little faster. All he knew was that this time it was going to end for good: no more shit was going to go down, his wife was going to be having HIS children and they WERE going to live happily ever after. *He hoped.*

They set off again at some speed, tearing down the motorway, passing signs for Birmingham, coming off at junction 2, then cutting through Halesowen and following the signs for Romsley. Frank slowed down, taking time to look around the unfamiliar territory. Jason had lured him to a place which he had no understanding of. He would struggle to find a way out quickly if it came to it. He noticed the scenery changing quickly, large houses and fields coming into sight. Jack glanced at the map and told him to take the next left up a country road, the destination under two miles away.

As they reached a secluded private road, Frank slowed down even further. Jack checked the address – they'd arrived. They'd begun the long drive up to the house when Jack spotted his father's car.

"He's here. That's his car."

Frank pulled up just behind it, wanting to dive out, run to the house and get his wife. But he did not know what lay behind those big doors. It was dark but a quick scan of the outside revealed extensive front windows and a large plot of land at the front. He could only imagine it was the same at the back. Loads of possible escape routes if Jason wanted.

Jack and Isobelle exit the car and Jack heads toward the house. Frank grabs hold of his arm.

"Don't do anything to jeopardise my wife."

"Whatever you may think, my father would not hurt her." He jerks his arm from Frank's grip and continues towards the house.

They ring the bell and wait... no answer, so Jack rings it again and this time uses the big door knocker as well. They see a light go on in the hallway and wait for the door to open. They all hear the click and Jason swings open the front door.

"Ah, the cavalry has arrived. Please come in." He smiles as if this were the norm.

Jack is the first to barge past his father and then Isobelle, leaving Frank behind. When Frank makes eye contact with Jason the look that passes between the two of them is lethal.

"If you..."

"See for yourself. She has not been harmed. I gave you my word."

Frank can hear Jack calling out for Autum which pisses him right off. He starts to walk a little quicker now as they all head straight for the dining room.

"Where is she?" Frank manages to speak first.

"She will be coming down soon; she went upstairs to get a blanket."...

Frank ran out of the room and headed for the stairs, shouting my name...

"Autum! Answer me, Autum!" I heard the voice I had so longed to hear. I came running out of my room, dropped the blanket and we both ran to each other. With one swoop, Frank lifted me up, twirled me around and kissed me like his life depended on it. Then as if in shock, he pulled away, put me down and started to pat me down to see if I was ok.

"Did he hurt you? Are you ok? God, I missed you so much."

Once he had got the last words out, he kissed me again, his tongue bursting through my lips more forcefully than before.

"Frank, I'm fine, honestly. Where are the others?" I managed to say once I'd got my breath.

"Downstairs."

Frank wrapped his arm around my shoulders and I put my arm around his waist as we headed downstairs. I could feel him staring at me from the corner of my eye, worry, relief and anger all showing. I wondered, could

Frank just walk away now he'd got me back? Can pigs fly? We both knew the answer to that.

"Don't do anything stupid," was the only thing I could say. He didn't answer.

As we entered the room, Frank released me even though I tried to hold onto his waist. Jack headed towards me.

"Thank God you're safe, did he...?"

"I'm fine, Jack, Jason did not hurt me, before you ask." By the time I'd blinked again, he had grabbed me in a bear hug and whispered into my ear,

"I couldn't live if anything happened to you."

I quickly pulled out of his hold. I tried to walk towards Frank but then Isobelle came into view. *I wish they would get out of the fucking way, Christ!* Then all three men left and headed into another room before I could speak. I think they wanted to give me and Isobelle space to talk. *Ironically...*

"I'm so glad that you're ok, Autum. It's been a long night for us all, we were so worried."

A hysterical laugh came out of my mouth so loud that she stopped and stared at me.

"Long night? What do you think it has been like for me? First I have had to put up with all this ex fiancé shit over the last few months and then, just when I think that my life is back on track, daddy dearest gets in on the act and drugs and kidnaps me. You sure have a way with words, Isobelle, such a way with words." I walk off.

"I came here because I was worried about you and that is how you speak to me? How dare you!"

Well you know where this is leading don't you...

I turn around and face her.

"How dare I? God, you're something else Isobelle. How dare you fuck up my life then think we can get back to normal?"

"But I thought we were..."

I start to poke her in the chest, "How dare you come here and act like you have come here with the best intention. You only came here to make sure that Jack isn't pining over me again. Scared of a little competition?" I poke her again.

I turn again to head towards Frank and the next thing I feel my hair is being pulled. I scream as I try to lessen the pain of my hair being yanked from my scalp.

"Aww you bitch!" I elbow her in the stomach. She let's go as I try to take a swing at her and miss, *damn, she's on form today.* She catches me right in the face. *The bitch has a good aim! She must be proud of that one but I'm not going to give her another chance. I never intended to have a fight but I think this is going to be a good one.* I charge at her and do a mad kind of monkey jump. She lands right on the floor, me pinning her down as I straddle her. The bitch slaps me so I go in, fists whirling. I hit the side of her jaw and she screams. She yanks my bloody hair again, bringing me down to her level then head butts me, making my vision blurred. I lose balance enough for her to push me off. She then kicks me in the stomach, *KICKS ME,* and I curl up in a ball feeling sick. She goes in for another shot and I grab hold of her ankle and bite it. She topples back and bangs her head. *It feels like we're fighting to the death.* There's no time to swap any more insults. It's down and dirty and I'm not going to lose, whatever happens. She's still recovering from her fall, so I take advantage and pin her down once again, each of us exchanging screeches. I must have missed a trick as her hands are around my neck like a woman possessed. All I can think of is how tight her grip is. I wrap both my hands around her wrists and focus on the look in her face. *She's enjoying this. And she's winning.* Her grip tightens, her victory feeding her strength. I have to think fast. I roll to the side then slam my knee into her groin. Yep, that does the trick. You see – women CAN feel pain just like men can. Needs must when you're being strangled...

She lets go of me, crying, screaming and shouting. I try to breathe, that's all, just try to breathe.

Then, the men (yes, do you remember them?) came running from out of the other room and pulled us apart.

"Well this has been an eventful evening, don't you think?" said Jason "I'd never have thought you had it in you. Either of you!" Before Jason could utter another word...

Frank lunged for him. "You son of a bitch!"

He caught Jason on his lip, cutting it and drawing blood. Jason wiped it away.

"I wondered when I would see the real you," said Jason, as Frank head butted him, sending him flying back.

To see two grown me in suits fighting is something else. Jason was much older than Frank but don't let his age fool you. He was fighting fit

126

and it was showing. They both swapped punches equally, to the face and stomach, uppercuts, even punches to the back. They didn't even look out of breath. As Frank forced Jason back and pinned him down over the table, Jack dived in: two against one. My head started to spin and I was crying out for them to stop, Isobelle smirking at my side. I hit her with a quick backhander and caught her nose which started to bleed, *bitch.*

I focused my energy on watching both father and son beat the hell out of my husband and all I wanted to do was help. A man's fist hitting me was something Miss Stubborn hadn't thought about when I got up and jumped on Jack's back. He reacted on instinct, smashing my face with the back of his head. If you have watched *The Matrix*, I was definitely going through that "slow-mo" where the hero bends to dodge the bullets with his leather coat and his bendy body. My version did not look so cool though. *I should stop watching those movies...* real life was showing me a rather different side. I was falling slowly back and losing consciousness.

I don't remember much and couldn't tell you how long I was out but when I came around I was upstairs in bed. My body ached liked never before and I could hardly move. I knew Frank was beside me as his gorgeous scent helped me open my eyes.

"Don't move, you've had a bit of a fall."

I wanted to laugh but the pain was telling me not to. I looked at Frank and my vision was ok but not great. He looked as bad as I felt. I tried to crack a joke.

"I hope you won." He didn't smile. He was getting a bruise over his left eye, his fists looked red raw and his suit needed replacing.

"I take it you lost then." I started to laugh and "pain" decided to punish me for it.

"You had us all worried for a moment."

"Only a moment? Must be losing my touch!"

"I want to take you to A & E to get you checked out."

"No, I'm fine. You, on the other hand..."

"I'm worried, Autum. You took a hit back there, knocked you out cold."

"And how do you think it will look when we turn up there? You looking like death and me looking like death's keeper."

"Didn't realise you could look worse than death."

"Tell my body that." And he finally cracked a smile, albeit a painful one, as he rubbed his jaw. "I will go in the morning. Right now, I cannot move. Not even an inch."

"Promise?"

"I promise, now get into bed and tell me you at least marked the bastards."

"What have I created?" Frank replied.

"A wife that will take no shit when her husband is being beaten up by two men."

"Should I be worried?"

"Only if I don't get sex on tap for all this pain. Not right now though." I laughed and "pain" punished me even more. Frank curled up beside me and, moaning with pain, we both fell asleep.

Jack and Isobelle crashed for the night in a room further down the hall.

"I'm proud of you, Isobelle." He kissed her on the lips.

"The bitch got lucky, that's all. What's with them two trying to bust people's noses?"

"Lucky shot, nothing more."

"Is your father ok?"

"I think so. I wanted to get you settled in first before I go and check on him."

"Go on, I will be fine. And Jack, your father will be proud of the way you stepped in tonight."

But as Jack headed downstairs, he thought to himself, *No, he'll probably say that he was coping well enough before I stepped in...*

Jason had moved to the lounge and had a glass in his hand and a decanter on the table; he looked up and beckoned to his son to join him.

"Whiskey?"

"Please, with ice." Jack sat down next to him.

"What a night, son." A chuckle left his mouth.

"Why did you take her, dad? The real reason." Jack had tried to find a reason in his own head for what his father had done but could think of none. He needed his father to tell him to ease his mind.

"I don't know what you mean."

"Frank told me you're in love with her, is that true?" A concerned look formed on his face.

"She was good for you, son, and you threw it all away. I love her, yes, but not in the way Frank thinks. She brought out my softer side and in a way I miss it. But you never told me she was a fighter. Well, they both are." He sipped his drink.

"Are you lonely, father?"

Jason turned to his son, unsure of why he would ask such a question.

"If you mean 'do I miss your mother?' then the answer is no. I have coped well over the years without that woman in my life. We both have. Once bitten, son, once bitten."

"But you and mum had a great relationship didn't you?"

"No son, we didn't. I…I kept the truth from you all these years because I knew how much you loved her."

Jack stood up.

"What do you mean? You kept the truth from me?"

"She wasn't a good mother."

"Liar!"

"I'm not lying, son. I don't expect you to understand what I am trying to say but she spent more of her time entertaining… others than she did looking after you." Jason looked up at his son and could see his chest rising and falling quickly.

"I don't believe you. She would never have done that."

"But she did and I was the one left to pick up the pieces. She left us both for someone with more money and a better lifestyle, one that did not involve a kid."

"Why are you telling me this now?"

"It just felt like the right time. I love you, son. I may be demanding and bad tempered but it took a talk with Autum for me to realise that I never really got over the way your mother left us. I threw myself into my work and shut out all of my close friends. They told me over and over again to leave her but I kept forgiving her each and every time until I could take it no longer and I threw her out."

"Did you stop her from seeing me?"

"Oh God no, she stop seeing you because she was too busy living the high life with a billionaire far richer than me. She was getting used to the party lifestyle and having a kid around would have spoilt all of that. I'm sorry you had to hear it like that."

Jack sat back down.

"Can things get any worse?" he said to his father.

Jason wrapped his arms around his son.

"I hope not, son."

"I love you, father."

Jason was touched by what his son had just said, something he would never have said openly before. They were both turning a corner and he knew that once things settled down, he would be spending more time in England with his son. And even though the name kept sticking in his throat, he knew that that would include Isobelle. They continued to embrace for some time before Jason replied.

"I love you too, son."

CHAPTER TWENTY

Frank and I started to stir around eight thirty. The pain had increased overnight and my body felt happier being dragged than walking freely. Each step towards the bathroom was like walking "the Green Mile". My head still hurt and I'd said that I was going to get checked out. I'd worry about any questions that were asked later. What I did know was that I was going to call the police. Yes, we had all got it out of our system the night before and I actually think that was probably what we all needed to do so that we could all move on, but there'd be no more presuming: it was going to end once and for all.

Jason would probably get a slap on his wrist and pay whatever he needed to so that nothing showed up on his record. He'd donate heaps of money to charity and walk away without a mark but I needed them to know that this nonsense had to stop and that I wouldn't put up with it any longer. *Remorse is a wonderful thing until you do it again.*

Everyone reached downstairs at roughly the same time; the half grins were given to each other, the visible bruises showing on everyone like trophy pieces. Jason had prepared a banquet for us all as if nothing had happened which took me back a bit. We all were famished though and I ate without much persuasion.

"I just wanted to say a few words to everyone," was Jason's opening line, "Firstly, I want to apologise to Frank and Autum for my behaviour. It was totally out of character and completely unacceptable. Whatever course of action they decide to take, I will accept."

I started to blush; it was as if he had read my mind and knew that I was going to call the police.

"Secondly, to my son, I'm sorry for the way things have turned out for you and how I have behaved but I hope that we have a future together. Isobelle, my words have been a little harsh but you make my son happy."

No apology then, Isobelle thought to herself.

I excused myself and headed for the lounge to make the call to the police.

"Are you ok?" Frank asked, rubbing my back.

"Yes, I won't be long."

Thank goodness for the guest book with the address underneath the picture promoting this place. I began to go through the events with the police in great detail and felt a weight was being lifted off my shoulders.

Jack gave Autum a sly look as she left the room. *She's up to something,* he thought, *I recognise the guilt on her face.* She had been gone less than two minutes when Jack asked if there was any more juice.

"Yes, do you want me to get some?" his father said.

"No, you sit down, I'll fetch it." He got up and left the room. He was heading back from the kitchen when he heard Autum talking. He crept to the doorway of the lounge, keeping himself out of sight. He couldn't hear all of the conversation but knew it involved his father. *Why has she mentioned his name?* He kept looking back to make sure that no one was looking for him but then he heard the words "statement" and "police station" and realised what was happening. *How could she do this to him after he had apologised, the bitch?* He didn't need to hear anymore, he was fuming. *No one is going to take my father away from me, NO ONE.*

He rejoined everyone and didn't speak.

"Are you ok, son? You seem upset."

It took all of Jack's will to act normal. He even put on a smile to mask his anger.

"Just thinking about more bacon," he said and everyone laughed.

"Do you want me to make some more?"

"No, this will do fine. Need to watch the waistline, you know." He patted his stomach, and continued to eat.

I didn't know how long I had been gone, but when I retuned everyone had finished eating.

"Your breakfast has gone cold; do you want me to make something fresh for you?"

This gesture made my guilt even harder to swallow. I needed to let Jason know what I had done and why. I didn't want him to find out when they were knocking on the door.

"Jason, can I have a quiet word please?" I was shaking like a leaf.

Frank stood up.

"Is something wrong?"

"No I just need to have a word with Jason, I won't be long."

Jack pushed his plate to the other side of the table and gave me the most evil look possible. It made me swallow, hard. He got up and left and I could feel the atmosphere change in an instant. I froze in my spot nearly forgetting what I wanted to tell Jason. As I started to walk, Jack appeared out of nowhere right in front of me. In one quick movement, he grabbed my hair and yanked me around so that I was facing everyone.

"Jack! What are you doing? You're hurting me!"

"Hurting you, you lying, scheming bitch."

Frank went to rush towards me then Jack surprised us all. He pulled out a knife and held it to my throat.

Isobelle started to scream. Jason was just stunned.

"What are you doing, son? Let her go, she's done nothing wrong."

"Tell them. Tell them all what you have just done."

Every time he moved my head my hair went with him causing me pain.

"I don't know what you're talking about!"

"Jack, let her go. Don't get yourself into anymore trouble," said Frank as he edged towards us. Jack backed up against the wall taking me with him.

"Tell them who you were calling when you left the room?"

My face started to heat with embarrassment; he must have overheard me somehow.

"I was going to tell you, Jason, that's why I wanted to speak to you."

"Tell me what?"

"I…I called the police." I looked over at Frank but his eyes were fixed on the knife at my throat. I could feel how hot Jack's breath was against my hair and my ear. "I'm sorry Jason I just had to."

"I understand, and you had every right to do so. Let her go, son, I deserve it."

"No, I won't have them take you away from me."

"Jack, listen. I don't know what she has said but we can work it out, I promise you. Now let her go."

"Give me your keys. NOW." He looked straight over to Frank.

"Never."

The knife pierced my skin, drawing blood. I started to cry and also started feeling sick, the headache coming back to me. I tried to relieve some of the tension he was putting on my hair but he just wrapped his hand around it even more so that when I tried to talk it was like I was being scalped.

"Give it to me now or I will kill her in front of you."

Frank threw him the keys.

"Don't do this, Jack. Please, she's not worth it," said Isobelle. But she knew that now there was no talking to him. The room had started to spin and I could feel breakfast rising up from my stomach. I started to wrench.

I called out Frank's name and threw up everywhere, Jack reacting and bending my head to the side.

"Jesus, Autum! What's wrong?"

"I don't know, I just don't feel right."

Isobelle came over to me.

"Jack, she doesn't look good."

"She's going nowhere without me." Jack's eyes were still fixed on Frank.

"Jack, if you let me go, I will call them and tell them that I have changed my mind and blew the whole thing out of proportion."

He twisted me to face him.

"I thought we had all turned a corner, but you just couldn't help yourself, could you?"

"I'm sorry, Jack, but I need to go to the hospital. I don't fell well. Please." And I threw up again. This time he did not have a chance to move and he got covered in sick.

"Bitch," he said but his grip remained firm.

"Take me, Jack," said Frank, "just let her get checked out. Your father can take her to the hospital, you can keep me here."

"You mean until the police arrive? Keys!"

I started to hold my stomach but my head was also hurting.

"God, man, look at her! She's sick!" The concern grew in Frank's voice.

For the first time, Jack realised that something was wrong. He loosened his grip on my hair.

"I'll drive and if you do anything stupid you will regret it, understood?" said Jack and started to move.

Frank would have agreed to anything as long as it meant Autum would get to go to hospital.

Jack turned to Isobelle.

"Do you still love me?" he said.

"Of course I do, you know that"

"Watch her in the back of the car. If she tries to do anything stupid, stab her."

"What? I can't, she's my best…"

"Friend? Is that what you were going to say. Remember how she treated you when you tried to make peace, remember how she looked at you with distaste, remember how she slapped you and threw food in your face then laughed at you. Is she your best friend now? Eh?" Without another word, to my shock and amazement, he pulled out a second knife and handed it to her.

Isobelle took it, with no hesitation.

"You've both gone mad," said Frank

"And who made us this way?"

"Frank, do as he says." My voice was weak. I just needed help.

"I can't let you do this, son."

"It's done, father." Jack headed towards the door, dragging me. Once the fresh air hit me the sickness got worse. I was in such excruciating pain I wanted to cry.

"Hurry, Frank." And with that, I was helped into the car by Isobelle, Jack and Frank who was seated in the front.

"Let me come with you," shouted Jason.

"No way," shouted Frank.

Frank was in a place he didn't know and relying on help he didn't want. He looked at his wife and saw the life draining out of her.

As the car started to move, Jack kept the knife pointed into Frank's side. I tried to sit up as much as I could and when I looked back towards the house, I could see Jason running towards his car. Jack was driving quite fast and every hump that we went over felt like I was being stabbed in the stomach.

"What's wrong with me?" Jack's foot pushed down on the accelerator.

"I don't know, darling, but we will have you checked out in no time."

"How touching," was Jack's reply.

We were about ten minutes into the journey when Isobelle started to talk to me.

"Why couldn't you just be my friend again? That's all I wanted."

"Do you really want to do this now?"

"Yes, I do."

"Well I don't. I'm too sick to have an argument with you, Isobelle. If you want me to be your friend, just shut the fuck up."

"Not the big shot now are you?"

"Just grow up, will you?" I moved away from her. I was sweating badly now as well as looking like shit, smelling of sick and hurting like mad. This day was going to be one to remember, even more so than last night. Well maybe not but still, one to remember.

"You took away all my friends..."

Yep, she still wanted to continue and I still wanted to ignore her.

"Look at me, bitch." She slapped me.

I was ill to the point that raising my hands to fight back was going to take effort. But I couldn't let her get away with that so with all my might I just screamed, grabbed her hair from both sides and the fight continued on from last night. I could feel the car swerving as Frank told us both to stop and Jack laughed as if this were some kind of joke.

Frank tried to reach over and pull us apart, only stopping when Jack prodded him with the knife. The hair pulling continued and Jack kept laughing and something snapped in Frank. *This prick is loving this far too much.* He smacked Jack hard in the face, the car swerved so much that the tyres screeched deafeningly and Isobelle and I stopped fighting.

Jack and Frank were now exchanging blows, Jack's hand leaving the wheel on more than one occasion.

"Stop it, you're going to kill us!" I shouted

"Jack, slow down!" Isobelle piped up.

Neither of them were paying attention to the road as they continued to swap blows. I tried to grab Jack from behind but Isobelle saw me move and pulled me back down. I told Frank to stop, for me. I told him how much I loved him and that what we had, Jack would never get. That seemed to do the trick. I felt I might not live to see another day and I needed him to know how much I loved him.

I started to drift off and could hear him yelling at me to keep awake. As I opened my eyes, I saw Frank crying, for me. I looked into the inside mirror and saw a smile on Jack's face and Isobelle shaking me to stay awake. Why? Probably so she could slap me again.

Despite all the noise and the shouting going on around me, my ears pricked up at a strange "click" sound. My eyes opened up a bit more. Why had no one else heard it? I had. I know I had. The car was now out of control, Jack driving like a mad man. Every time I looked up I could see his stare and his smile. *He was going to kill us all.*

I looked behind me to see Jason still trying to keep up with us. Frank was still leaning over holding my hand and even Isobelle had started to cry too.

"Stop him. Please, Isobelle. He will only listen to you."

"Why should I help you?"

"Because if you do, I will say you had no involvement in this. I swear." I could see Isobelle pause, thinking about what I said.

"Please, Isobelle."

She undid her seatbelt and leaned forward. Frank went to undo his own but found it was already off. He looked up at Jack, who turned and smiled at him. Frank did not have time to deal with him; he needed to make sure that I stayed awake.

"Move over and swap seats," he shouted to Isobelle. Jack swerved the car, knocking Isobelle back and sending Frank flying into the passenger door hitting his head on the window.

"Put your seatbelt back on, Frank, please!" I screamed. Jack swerved the car to the right before Frank could grab hold of the belt. Isobelle tried her hardest to hold on herself and managed to strap herself back in. My neck was being pushed to the limit with the seatbelt locking me in place over and over again.

"Seatbelt Frank, quickly!" The only thing I saw was the gleam in Jack's eye. I looked from him to the road then to Frank before we hit something with such force that I felt like my chest, neck and stomach were being sliced in half. I screamed along with Isobelle as Frank's body hit the windscreen and rolled over the bonnet onto the grass verge. The car came to a halt.

The horn was blaring in the background. Jack's head had hit the airbag, knocking him out cold. I couldn't see much and started to go into shock. I looked at Isobelle whose lifeless body lay slumped, blood splattered along the window and down the side of her face. I couldn't react, couldn't speak and couldn't move. My thoughts returned to Frank, the love of my life, lying outside of the car. I didn't know if he was alive or dead. I started shaking some more and heard Jason outside the car trying to open it. I looked over to my right as he ran onto the verge and bent down; I still couldn't see properly. He was down there for ages so I knew it wasn't good. When he re-appeared he was covered in blood and I could feel the tears running down my eyes, still motionless.

I heard sirens getting louder and louder and then there were helmets and uniforms blocking my view of where Frank was laying. I turned again as the firemen told me to stay calm and that they would get us out in no time. There was still no movement from Isobelle or Jack. I started to move my mouth and at first no words came out. I tried again. I called out for Frank and it came out as a whisper with all the noise around me. *Why haven't they carried him away yet?* But in my heart, I was certain it was because he was already dead. I felt the cold rush of air hit me as I was gently carried out of the car. How could I have not noticed when they cut me out? I didn't even notice anyone around me but I was glad I was free. As I was carried away on a stretcher and in a neck brace, I called out for Frank and tried to point to the floor.

"We're doing all we can," someone said as I was hoisted up into the ambulance. The door shut. The pain started to kick in again and I felt that I need to go to the toilet. The toilet, for goodness' sake! I tried to remain calm. I needed to, for Frank. I wanted my mum and dad, Rebecca – anyone in fact so that I wouldn't be alone. I wanted to close my eyes, I was getting tired, the tears stinging my face. *Just let me close them for a few minutes and then I will wake up.*

When I opened my eyes, I was in a hospital bed, a monitor hooked up to my finger and a drip in my arm. I noticed Jason asleep on the chair next to me holding my hand. I pulled it away and mumbled Frank's name. He sat up.

"Thank God you're awake."

"Frank. Where is he? What are you doing here?" My mouth was dry and my voice hoarse.

I tried to move but my body kept me firmly in place.

"Is he dead?" I couldn't believe what I was saying but I needed to find out. I could feel myself slipping back into sleep and I needed to know quickly.

"I have contacted your parents, they are on their way." I fought to sit up again as he rushed to support my head with pillows.

"You need to rest; the doctors will be in shortly to check on you."

"Tell me God damn it, is he dead?"

I saw Jason rise, his expression suddenly changing and my heart sank.

"He's in a coma."

My eyes closed immediately after that, my brain didn't want me to hear anymore.

Chapter Twenty One

Jack slowly stirred out of his sleep. He had no idea what had happened when he crashed Frank's car. He look around to see where he was... *Hospital.* He never thought he would survive the crash and he hadn't wanted to. He had lost everything and he wanted everyone to suffer even if that meant losing Autum. Her image entered his mind and he needed to know where she was. But he couldn't move. His left wrist hurt when he tried to move it and he realised that he was handcuffed to a rail. He looked at his whole body. It was badly bruised and his chest hurt. When he reached up to touch his head, he noticed that it had been bandaged. He leaned to one side and felt for the buzzer to call for attention.

A nurse rushed in and he asked for water. She poured out a glass and held it to his mouth with a straw so he could take small sips.

"The people that came in with me. Are they ok?"

The nurse replied only that he should rest and that the police were outside and might come in later to see him.

"Police?" he was genuinely at a loss why the police would want to speak to him.

"You've had quite a knock to the head," she said in a chirpy voice as she checked the monitor. She checked his chart then went to leave the room.

"Wait..." She quickly turned around. "I need to call my father, his name is...."

"He has been here since you came in. He has been visiting..." She cut off her own sentence and left the room abruptly.

Jack leaned back and closed his eyes to think. He was weak and in pain. Then the door burst open.

"How could you, son? You fucking idiot! Was it your intention to kill everyone? WAS IT?" Jason didn't mean what he said but he was mad.

His father was shouting. *He didn't even ask me how I was...* "Glad you're alive, son. Are you hurt?" *Nothing. He must have been in before to see me as he didn't even bat an eye lid that my wrist was cuffed.*

"Is she alive? The nurse wouldn't tell me anything."

Jason ran his hand through his hair, frustrated, before he took a seat by his son's bed.

"Isobelle suffered..."

"Not Isobelle," he shouted, "Autum! I need to know if she...she is alive."

"She's stable. She was taken into surgery, came out after a few hours and I left her sleeping."

"Please, I need to see her, to..."

"No, son. Nothing you can do now will undo the harm you have done. At no point have you even asked about Isobelle – your girlfriend. Remember her? Well she's due to be released tomorrow, they think. Just in case you were going to ask," Jason said sarcastically.

"There's no need for that. Of course I was going to ask if she was ok. You just never gave me the chance. I'm glad she's ok. How long have you been here?"

"Two days."

"What? How can that be?"

"Listen, son, I will do what I can but the police want to speak to you. It's Frank. He's in a bad way... he's in a coma."

Jack couldn't take it all in. What a mess, what a bloody mess he had created and he knew that this time even his father couldn't fix it. He wanted to say something but no words could form in his mouth and when he tried again the police walked in.

Jason immediately got up to greet the officers as they explained to his son that they needed to ask him a few questions. Jack looked at his father and nodded.

"I'm staying," Jason said and took a seat again as the officers took out their notepads and started to write. Jason listened in great detail to his son confessing what he had done. It made him sick to the bone and he realised that his son might actually need help. It was breaking his heart but he still had to be there for him. He would still do whatever it took to keep his son out of jail even though he knew a sentence would be inevitable.

I woke again and didn't know if it was night or day or how long a time I had been sleeping. All I knew was that the pressure in my head had gone. I went to rub my temple and felt the dressing around my head. I looked around for the buzzer to call the nurse. When she arrived, I asked about my husband.

"How is he? I need to see him." I started to sit up, pain not registering in my mind, and flipped my feet off the bed.

"Mrs Howard, you cannot get up. Let me call in the doctor, you're not in any fit state to get up." She pushed my feet back into the bed.

"He needs me." I felt sleepy again. *God, please keep me awake,* I thought, *I need to get this drip out of my arm.* I tried to pull it out.

"What are you doing?" the nurse cried out and shouted for help. *Like I'm in any state to attack her...* Two doctors rush in as they hold me down by both arms.

"I need to see my husband; he needs to know that I am here."

"In good time, Mrs Howard. You have taken a bit of a beating by all accounts," said one of the doctors, releasing me and looking at a chart. "You have internal injuries. We had to operate to relieve some of the swelling around your brain and your left eye is swollen. And I'm afraid we have some worse news... we tried everything we possibly could to save the baby but you were haemorrhaging when you were bought in. You'd lost a lot of blood..."

I paused for a moment, stuck in time, processing everything that the doctor had just said.

"What did you just say? Are you telling me that I was pregnant?"

"I'm sorry... we couldn't save the baby," the doctor repeated, "I will see what we can do about taking you to see your husband but you need to prepare for the worse. He was in surgery for several hours to stop the bleeding in his brain"

I felt lost. Not only had I been pregnant but now I had lost the baby I never even knew I had. I felt down at my stomach and said sorry in my mind for all the misery that I had caused my unborn child. *Maybe that kick to the stomach had done the damage but I couldn't blame Isobelle. Neither of us had any idea.*

I snapped myself out of my mood – I could weep for my loss later. For now, Frank was somewhere in this hospital, alone and not hearing his wife's voice. I needed to leave and see him no matter what greeted me. Nothing could be worse than all the feelings stirring in my head right now.

"Please," was all I could muster.

The doctors looked at each other, then one spoke.

"We will get a wheelchair for you but you must take it easy. You need a lot of rest as you will be in here for a few weeks. Understood?" They left and the nurse helped me swing my feet around. She steadied my pain filled body so that I could stand up but my feet gave way as I tried to hold onto the nurse. A wheelchair came in soon afterwards and I sat down. I was pushed along, the drip still in my arm, down a long corridor and through several doors until we came to a standstill outside another door. I was turned round and wheeled through backwards and when I was righted, the sight in front of me made me gasp. Tears started flowing freely down my face as I was wheeled closer to the bed. Frank looked like he was sleeping and at peace. His head was bandaged and he had tubes in his mouth and arms but it was the loudness of the machine bleeping at me that made the whole scene feel real. I reached out to take his hand which was still soft to the touch. The faint smell of his aftershave drifted up to my nose.

"Talk to him. He can still here you. I will leave you alone but not for long" And with that, the nurse left the room.

I tried to be brave but when I looked again at the tubes and the machine and felt the eerie atmosphere of the room, I burst out crying.

"I'm so sorry, Frank. I caused all of this. Don't leave me. Please, I love you so much, please don't leave me. I need you now more than anything." I kiss his hand, I promise I will give up work and be the perfect housewife. *Anything. Just wake up.* I bend down, lie my head on his bed still holding his hand and fall asleep.

I hear voices and ignore them. *They're in my head.* I hear them again and slowly open my eyes.

"Mum? Dad?" *When did I get back to my room?*

"Oh baby, we thought we'd lost you," says my mother, piling kisses all over my face.

"You gave us such a scare young lady," adds my father, trying his best to hold back his feelings. I reach out and he grabs my hand.

"Sorry dad, sorry for everything."

"This is not the time for talking, just rest. We will be here when you wake up."

"Frank..."

"We know. He is getting the best help possible. Let them take care of him, you need to be strong for him when he wakes up."

"I need to tell you both something. I… I lost our baby. It's my fault and I wish I never met Jack. This is all because of him and Frank has paid the price. We all have." I'm blabbering but I don't care.

"Shush now, whatever has happened, it's over now. We will deal with this another day." Both mum and dad look at each other, convincing no one that this is over, least of all me.

I hear a knock at my door and see Elena and James walk in, Frank's parents. *How the hell can I face them after what I have put their son through?*

They greet my parents and I sit up, searching for something to say.

"Sorry this hasn't happened under better circumstances," is all I can think of. I try and fight back the guilt I am feeling as they tell us how Frank has been getting on.

Nearly three weeks passed and I was now due to be released from hospital. Frank was showing signs of improvement and I stayed by him every day until I was told to leave or get some sleep or to eat. Whenever that happened, his parents took over and so it went on. The thought that I would be leaving felt strange.

Jason came to me to tell me that Jack was still in and was asking for me. Isobelle had been discharged some weeks ago but had remained by his side every day. Apparently, she was asking for me too. *I bet she was.* I ignored everything I heard. Jason's presence just told me that the police had done *nothing*. When I smiled and excused myself, he told me that Jack was being charged for reckless driving.

"Why don't we up that to murder since he killed my unborn child?" The words choked me as I spoke them.

"You were pregnant?"

"Yes I was." I stormed off, Jason calling out my name.

Fucking "reckless driving"! Can you believe that? I stormed back to my room and told both my and Frank's parents. *This wasn't over, not by a long shot.* I couldn't believe it. He had kidnapped me, held me at knifepoint then tried to kill three people by crashing a car. And he'd been done for *reckless driving*. No justice, no justice whatsoever. I couldn't go on like this anymore, that was for sure. I had changed inside but not for the better. This time I needed to be the one who ended it. I just didn't know how.

After my release, Frank's parents got him moved to a hospital near our home. Once they found out about the baby, they started fussing over me. I still hadn't really grieved for my loss because I hadn't had the time. Frank and the family filled all of my thoughts and I was glad. My parents stayed on for another two weeks along with Elena and James and then they all went back home. I kept them informed daily but it was nice having all the family together and Rosetta loved cooking for so many people. Rebecca came to visit along with the girls but I wasn't sure if they were just there for back-up. I told her everything was cool and about the baby and I also told her that I wasn't going to hide or live the rest of my life looking over my shoulder. No matter where I was, if Jack or Jason wanted to get to me, they would.

Isobelle was torn on what to do next. She had never seen this side of Jack before, *a man possessed,* but she also knew that she would not abandon him either. When she found out about the baby, she felt bad that the kick she gave Autum could have triggered things off... *Did she blame me? Would she have fought me knowing she was pregnant? I don't think so. Autum had put out a restraining order on Jack but would that stop him seeing her again? I doubt it. He had been very quiet since we got home. He hardly spoke most days and just kept apologising for what he had done. Maybe this was his turning point. His father wanted him to spend some time with him in America but he refused, said he still had unfinished business. That made me worry. We didn't hear much about Frank or how he was doing. All I hoped was that he would recover.*

CHAPTER TWENTY TWO

I was at work three months after the crash when I got a call from the hospital to say that Frank had woken up. I dropped everything and drove like a maniac, unsure how I arrived without actually killing anyone. I was ushered through the wards immediately. I stopped outside his door and paused. It was silly really but I was so scared at the thought of what I would find.

"Does he know who I am?"

"He was asking for you," the doctor replied putting his hand on my shoulder. Then he opened the door for me.

I entered the room. The machines seemed quieter this time around. Frank was lying down and it was only when I approached the bed that he turned to face me. I slumped in the chair as he reached out his hand for me to take. Tears left me and he reached up to wipe them.

"Sorry Frank, for everything."

"How long have I been here?" he asked and I filled him in on everything except the loss of our child. He was recovering and I did not want to add that to the chain of events as well. We talked for what seemed like hours, the time had flown by. Then the doctor came in for me to let him rest.

"Will he be ok, doc?"

"He will make a full recovery in time; he will need plenty of rest and care."

I knew that wouldn't be a problem, as I had already decided to take leave and look after him. I owed him that much at least and the more I thought about being a stay at home wife, the more I was getting around to the idea.

"Do you know when I can take him home?"

"We would like to monitor him for another week at least but after that, if we are happy with his progress, then you should be able to take him home."

I kissed the doctor on the cheek as this was the best news I'd ever heard. I was going to return later on and I wanted to give Frank's parents the good news.

I left the hospital with a smile on my face speaking on the phone to James and Elena, and not looking where I was going. I bumped into someone and apologised immediately until I heard that familiar voice. I froze, unable to look into his eyes... Jack. I took a few steps back as he approached me.

"What are you doing here?" I said, angry and shocked.

"I still have to come for checkups," Jack replied, "I never meant for any of this to happen."

"You're a fucking liar, Jack. Everything you do is because you want something, now get out of my way."

He blocked me so I slapped him and moved past.

"I heard about the baby," he shouts and I stop. I can sense his eyes boring into the back of me. I take a deep breath as I grind my teeth in anger and continue to walk away. Little do I know he's right behind me. I reach my car, pull out my keys and open the door but he grabs my arm and pushes me into the passenger side. I start to kick and scream but he tells me to shut the fuck up and put my belt on or he'll hurt Isobelle. I stop for a split second as he starts the car, unsure if this is a bluff. *Why should I care?* I shouldn't but I do.

"I'm tired of this Jack, you can't keep doing this. What do I have to do to get you to stop?"

He continues to drive without saying another word.

"Where is Isobelle? Haven't you done enough to me already?" I grab the steering wheel and the car starts to swerve.

"What the hell do you think you are doing?" he says, pushing me back, "Do that again you silly bitch and this time you will not live."

I have nothing left to lose. Slowly, I put my hand around the handle so that I can open the door. I forget that I've put my belt on. I don't get far.

"What the......?" He pulls the car over and looks at me. "Shut it."

I shout and scream to get some attention but even though people hear, no one comes to help me. He grabs my clothes and draws me back in.

"What happened to you Autum? You used to be such a good girl. Now shut the door."

But I'm not going to be a good little girl. I fold my arms across my chest as hate starts to build up inside me, so much that even I don't recognise what's coming over me.

Jack starts to tut at me and I ignore him.

"SHUT IT!" he shouts and twists my right arm so hard I think he's going to dislocate my shoulder. I scream out for him to stop as I reach for the door and slam it shut, the pain shooting up my arm.

Jack continues to drive and I try to reach for my phone in my pocket. *Please don't ring, please.*

I pull it out, still with my arms crossed and pretend that I am looking out of the window. I press on Rebecca's name and wait for her to answer. I look forward again and try not to draw any attention, then I look back down and hear her faint voice. I start to talk loudly to Jack, hoping she can hear me, thanking my stars that my phone is still on silent from my visit to Frank.

"Jack, you cannot keep kidnapping me. I bet there is nothing wrong with Isobelle, you just said that for me to co-operate, didn't you?" He says nothing.

"You need to say your goodbyes, Autum."

"What do you mean goodbyes? Are you going to kill me?" I start getting hysterical. Jack just continues to drive.

I hope that Rebecca is still on the line as I feel the phone drop from my hand; I kick it under the seat and he looks over but says nothing. The drive continues for another forty-five minutes and he turns off onto a dirt track road. My heart starts to palpitate. *This is it. No Frank. No babies. No goodbyes.*

"Get out."

I start to shake and refuse to budge.

"Don't do this Jack, please, I don't want to die."

He gets outs of the car and comes round to my side. I try to unbuckle quickly and move over but he grabs me and pulls me out, kicking and screaming.

"Jack, please!" The tears flow freely down my face. He continues part dragging me up a hill towards a huge disused building. *Oh God, no one will ever find me.* I continue to fight him as much as possible.

"Save your energy, you're going to need it," he laughs.

We get inside. I'm unsure what it was used for but there are so many different rooms, metal stairwells and graffiti everywhere. For all I know, there could be drug users and tramps using this as a place to stay. We climb three floors and I hear muffled noises, yes voices, which means there is more than one person here. Jack continues forward until I see a room ahead. I can't speak, I'm too stunned. *This is my final resting place.* I am jolted out of my shock when he throws me into a room and I skid across the floor. I protect my head by using my hands to take the brunt of it and get grazes all up my arm, blood spilling and bits sticking to my skin. I look up to see Isobelle and, more shockingly, my mum and dad. I turn around and look up at him before I charge. He isn't expecting it and I hit him with a right hook. He falls back a little and starts to laugh.

"Is that the best you can do? It wasn't hard persuading mummy and daddy that I had taken you." He laughs again.

I run back towards my family to try to untie the rope he had used to bind them to a pillar. He see's my intention and charges at me as I head towards my father. As I dive towards him and start to untie his bonds, I get dragged away by Jack. I tilt my head towards him and kick him in the head.

"Bitch!" He let's go and I charge again to my father. I manage to reach him for a few seconds, just enough to loosen the robe and for my father to try and do the rest.

Jack grabs me and pulls me upright by my hair. He holds me up in front of my father, his breathing heavy and ragged.

"I love your daughter and this is how she treats me. You see, Autum, everything I did was because of you. My life cannot exist without you. I thought I could move on but I was kidding myself, my father and especially you Isobelle." He turns me to face her.

"Let me go, Jack." I struggle in his hold.

"I told her that this was goodbye." He swings me round and kisses me on the lips.

I wipe my mouth and spit at him. He smirks as he wipes his face, then he walks me over to my father. I start to cry. I tell him how much I love him and that when he walked me down the aisle it was the happiest day of my life. He mumbles as tears start to fall. Jack moves me to my mother and I tell her that I am so proud to be her daughter, how much I love her and that I am sorry that she will never see her grandchild. By the time I reach Isobelle I'm a sobbing wreck. I tell her that I'm sorry how things turned out between us, that all the things I did were because of what she had done to me. I apologise that our friendship has come to this and because I can't take back what has happened. I tell her I hope that she can forgive me in time. Jack starts to move backwards taking me with him.

I shout over to my dad, as my time on this earth comes to an end,

"Tell Frank I will always love him and that whatever happens to me, he must move on and love again. Tell him that I am sorry that I lost our child and wish I had a second chance." My throat is blocked and I can't speak anymore. I'm dragged further and further away from my family and my friend.

"How touching," says Jack and pretends to wipe a tear from his eye.

I look around for something to grab onto and try and clutch hold of a pillar for support. I am *not* going to die no matter what. I can see my father struggling, more frantic now. Jack releases my hair to untie my hands and I start to run. He chases me and I look around for anything I can use as a weapon. I spot some type of piping. He spots it too and sees me heading for it. I can feel him trying to grab me and spot how close he is out of the corner of my eye. I run and pick up the pipe not realising how heavy it is. It nearly pulls me down but I use both hands to hold it, grabbing and swinging at the same time. I hear a thud and realise Jack has been hit. He falls to the floor, blood seeping from a wound to the head. I drop the pipe and grab my hair and scream hysterically. *I have just committed murder.* I fall onto my knees in front of him and shake him over and over again.

"Don't do this to me, Jack!" He doesn't move.

I hear muffled screams as I look up and see my family still struggling to release their binds. I walk over to them like a zombie.

I release my father first. He rips off the tape around his mouth and hugs me. I give no response. He releases my mum and then Isobelle and they all crowd around me, my arms still at my side, shock setting in. I take a look over my shoulder again and Jack is still lying there.

"I'm so sorry Isobelle; he was going to kill me."

"It's ok, it's ok." She strokes my hair away from my face as a mother would for a child who is upset.

"Let's get her out of here," my father says, "We will call an ambulance as soon as we can."

We start to walk out, my father holding me close, my mother consoling Isobelle. We head out of the room and start to walk down the corridor when we all hear a screeching sound. We look round to see Jack charging. *Impossible!* I don't react. *I killed him. Who is this madman running at me?* By the time I've blinked, my dad has been knocked aside, hit by the same pipe I hit Jack with. *He didn't stand a chance.* I watch him fall and look up again to see Isobelle has blocked the path to me. *She is protecting me from Jack.* He continues to charge like a bull and yet I can't move. All the noises are mixing in my head, the cries and screams, and yet Jack is not letting up. He raises the pipe to swing at Isobelle, his eyes still fixed on me. I push her out the way and duck as he swings. Jack is unstable so when Isobelle's composed herself she grabs his ankle and he loses his balance. He grabs my clothing and pulls me down with him. He drops the pipe and tries to crawl up to the rest of my body as I struggle to free myself from his weight on top of me. His head wound is more noticeable the closer he gets.

"Couldn't you just love me?" His voice is weak and he keeps shaking his head. *He's trying to remain conscious.*

I beat at his shoulders.

"Get off me, Jack." Fear laces my voice.

"Just tell me you love me, Autum. Just one more time. You know I will always come back to you. Always."

He may be ready to pass out, I don't know, but as I look at him I know for his own piece of mind, he *needs* to hear it. And if he believes it, then maybe we can all leave here alive.

"I love you, Jack." My voice is shaky but calm. I pause for a moment then say it again, "Jack, I love you."

As I lift up his head and brush away the blood soaked hair in front of his face, I find myself asking him, "What went wrong?" He looks up at me, his breathing intermittent against my chest.

"I realised I could never give you up, Autum, never. I loved you the first time I laid eyes on you and I will love you with my last breath. I did what I did because I thought I could get you back. There will never be anyone else who understands me like you do. I tried my best with Isobelle," and he tilts his head to look at her, "but I could never love her like I love you."

"Jack, please."

He blinks slowly but each blink takes slightly longer. He opens his mouth to speak but smiles up at me first.

"Thank you," he says, his voice but a whisper, "Tell my father... I'm sorry."

I feel his chest rise for what feels like forever then fall, never to rise again. I watch his eyes close and his hands fall gently to my side.

I let out the loudest scream ever to be heard as I sob uncontrollably. I continue to stroke Jack's hair until I feel someone take hold of my hand mid-stroke. It's Isobelle, her mascara and foundation all mixed together streaming down her face. But that isn't what catches my attention when I look up at her. It's her eyes... The eyes of a woman hell bent on revenge.

About the Author

A first time author living in Birmingham, England. I spent my early years touring Britain with a theatre company pursuing my then passion for Amateur Dramatics. I now enjoy organising Black Tie Events for children's charities and in my spare time I enjoy entertaining family and friends.

Lightning Source UK Ltd.
Milton Keynes UK
UKOW02f1813010615

252696UK00001B/65/P